THE DIARIES OF SYRA BOND

by

SYRA BOND

I0517489

Published by **CHIMERA**
ISBN 9781780806020

CHAPTER 1

At first I could not write it down; it was all too embarrassing and I was ashamed. When he came to see how much I had written and realised I had done nothing, he bound my ankles even more firmly. He did not speak, but I could sense his impatience as he pulled the thin ribbon tight and I knew he would not tolerate any more delay. He nodded, and I knelt obediently down on all fours. He faced my feet, wrapped his left arm around my waist to lift me slightly off the floor, and laid the flat of his right hand against my taut buttocks. The warmth of his palm against my skin as he caressed it made me moan in anticipation of my punishment. As he drew his hand away, and brought it back down with a stinging smack, I clenched my teeth and swallowed a scream.

When he finished spanking me until my bottom was a flaming red, he let me slip from his crooked arm and I lay on the floor, panting. He looked into my eyes as though trying to see if I was containing my pain, but I did not feel any pain. I knew he could see nothing in my eyes except eagerness for more. I thought of asking him for a brighter light, but I did not dare. He would be angry if I spoke without being given permission, and it would be obvious to him I was trying to put off doing what he told me to do. Already he knows me too well. No, I will make do with the light I have been given. Just before he closed the door I thought of trying to slacken the rope around my ankles, and as I squirmed my legs against its tension I felt a twinge of pain that was strangely comforting. The quick, penetrating jab of sensation against my skin reminded me of what I have been trying to forget. It reminded me of what I have to write...

I cannot remember exactly when it all began. It does not really matter, I suppose. It all began about a year ago, I think, although it seems longer. So much has happened since I first met him, it is as though a whole lifetime has been squeezed into a few months. Since he found me - because that is what happened, he found me - events have become confused in my mind. But I will try to get it right, as I dare not do otherwise. He says he will check on my work every day from now on and if it is not up to his standards - and I know how high they are - he will punish me. Sometimes I wonder if I can stand another beating. It was different in the beginning; the mere thought of a cane's cruel lick or of a hand's hot smack sent me into a delirium of anticipation. It was a beautiful relief, the deep inner sensation of pain and the engulfing waves of humiliation accompanying it, but now I really do not feel anything any more...

I was a postgraduate student in psychology and getting on well with my research. My main interest was sensory deprivation and the recent work of Professor Rivero Lange of the University of Seville. His studies concentrated on the individual's response to fear and how it ties in with sexuality and sensory deprivation. I was reading something he had written about how far we can push ourselves into danger against our better judgement; how far we dare go even in the face of our darkest fears. He undertook close analysis of his test subjects, their limits and their breaking points. It seemed exciting work and I wanted to know more. I wrote to him and told him about some of my own ideas along the same lines, but he never replied.

Then one day my supervisor, Dr Max Baal, a well known psychologist and an expert on the treatment of people who have been brainwashed, told me I looked tired and suggested I take a week off. He was right. I felt jaded and needed some sunshine. He said he had a friend who owned a small apartment on the *Costa del Sol*, and before I had time to think about it he arranged for me to stay there.

When I arrived in Spain it was hot, *too* hot. I had not expected the intense sunlight, and before I even got to the apartment I felt faint. A craggy-faced old woman met me at the door. She was cloaked in black and jangled a heavy bunch of keys in her bony hand. It was a ground floor flat; part of an old house squeezed into a jumble of white, thick-walled buildings, but inside it was spacious and cool.

The old woman shook the handle of a door leading from the hall that was padlocked. 'Locked,' she said emphatically. 'Doctor not here. *Locked*.'

I shrugged as she handed me a single key, pointed to the bathroom, and left.

I threw my bag down on the bed, opened the French doors and stepped out into a small, high-walled garden. A stone bench with flowers growing at its base sat against one wall, and opposite it a large grey wooden door was set into the bleached bricks. A terracotta pot with bright red flowers decorated a small metal table in the centre of the garden. I do not have to close my eyes to see it again, the scene is so vivid. I could feel the breeze drifting up from the sea, wafting through the tight rows of whitewashed houses in soft, billowing waves and bathing me in its humid warmth. I sat on one of the flimsy metal chairs beside the table and opened my legs wide. My thin cotton panties were damp with perspiration. I love the feeling of salty moisture wetting the gusset of my panties, the way the material tugs gently at my pussy whenever I move, and the way the sticky tension parts my labia and exposes my delicate inner flesh. Without thinking, I prized the edges of the flimsy fabric away and felt the warmth of my flesh against my fingertips. I looked around me, and suddenly saw a man standing on a balcony in one of the cluster of adjoining houses. He was wearing a bright red and white Hawaiian shirt, and the contrast of the bold, jumbled pattern against the whitewashed buildings was intensified by the bright sunshine as he leaned over the black ornamental railing. I knew he realised I had seen him and I felt excited by his penetrating stare.

I lowered my head and rested my chin against the top of my chest. I tried to look shy, as though I was going to remove my hand from between my legs, get up and walk away, but I was really concentrating on the glistening pinkness of my flesh where I had pulled my panties aside. I stared at my labia and felt the touch of the man's eyes. I was not embarrassed, I was only aware of being careful not to rush and disappoint him. I knew I was being watched, and it was as though his prying eyes were a gift; his presence forced me to take my time and very slowly and gently press my fingertips against my clitoris. Then I slipped two fingers into the warm depths of my rosy slit. Such delicate moisture, such satiny wetness, so silky it let my fingers slip with ease between my soft flesh as I sat back and opened my legs even wider.

I would recognise again that figure on the balcony by his garish shirt and his shock of black hair, but once I had seen *him* I always recognised him the same way I know my own fingers and pussy. Did it matter that I spread my thighs wide that afternoon and pulled the edges of my white panties away from my sex? Of course it did. I know I should never have leaned back and stiffened my legs and brought them together as I pulled my panties down around my thighs. I should never have twisted the material into a thin, cutting rope and rolled it slowly across the tops of my thighs as though binding myself. I should not have moaned so loudly as the heat of the sun against my perspiring skin made my labia swell and throb against my fingertips. I should not have opened my mouth as I felt the surge of tension making me stretch my toes out in an uncontrollable spasm and forcing my ankles out so straight they ached. I should never have lifted my hips as high as I could so the man on the balcony could clearly see the blooming lips of my vulva responding to his scrutiny.

But I did.

I opened myself to him; I showed him my pussy in all its glory while sitting in that sunlit garden as though it was just another innocent flower. I showed him how I brought myself close to orgasm and then held back so I could start all over again, writhing on the chair as I teased myself, holding on to those moments of delectable anticipation. Then, when I finally let go, I stretched myself out for him, my whole body jerking and quivering while I looked up at him as though it was he driving me past the brink.

No, I should never have done those things. If I had not done them, then I would not have felt the way I did later when I wandered down to a nearby cafe for a drink. I would not have felt so electrified, so aroused, so available, and perhaps, just perhaps, *he* would not have been able to capture me so easily.

The first time I saw him he was with his other pet. I call her the pet because that is how he used to refer to me as well. 'Syra, my pet,' he would say whenever he came up behind me and squeezed my neck. 'Syra, my pet,' he would say when he was instructing me and wanted me to stand with my arms by my side and listen carefully. 'Syra, my pet,' he would say when he thought I had disobeyed him and he needed to reprimand me. Even so, I believe I always thought of her as the pet even before I heard him call me that. She was taller than me and very slender. She was beautiful, I suppose, though I could never have admitted it at the time. Yes, she was beautiful and I was jealous of her straightaway. I can see her now just as I saw her that first time - a haughty pampered bitch, a dark poodle prancing along with her nose in the air and her leash dangling loosely from the collar around her throat. She *was* like a poodle, so obedient she did not have to be restrained.

He - this unknown beautiful stranger - walked across the cafe with the pet hanging on his arm. He was so handsome everyone looked at him. There was something about him that drew people's attention, just as it captured mine like a magnet. I immediately liked the shape of his nose, narrow and long, his golden

4

tan, his long black hair and his muscular arms tipped with manicured fingernails. I smelled the pet's perfume, a sharp, citrus-like scent, and wrinkled my nose to convey my contempt for her. She did not see me surreptitiously sneering at her, but I did not care.

I felt nervous as they walked behind me. I should have known then, I suppose. That slight feeling of fear should have warned me. I felt him stop walking and knew he was looking at me; I could feel his eyes. I had draped my hair over my left shoulder and I could feel his stare on the nape of my neck. His regard was almost as hot as the sun's and made me feel a delicious prickling between my shoulder blades.

'Syra,' he said abruptly.

'Sorry?' I turned around in my chair. I should not have turned around. I know that now. It was the last time I had control of my life. That pathetic 'sorry' was the last word I uttered before I was enslaved.

'Why are you sorry?' he asked me very seriously. 'What have you done?'

'I don't know... nothing,' I replied feebly. 'I think you have me confused with someone else. My name is...'

'Syra,' he said emphatically. 'You could be no one else but Syra. Syra, my pet, I am not confused. May we sit with you?' He pulled a chair out for the pet and then sat down opposite me without waiting for my consent. The pet wriggled herself down onto the chrome strips of the shiny metal chair, and I inhaled her scent again.

'Eve,' she said in a low, even voice, grudgingly introducing herself to me.

Suddenly there was a commotion and a waiter came rushing towards us waving a towel, flicking it wildly at the customers as though he had gone mad and was hallucinating a world full of threatening wasps. '*Senor! Senor! Una bomba! Una bomba!*' he shouted. '*Senor, una bomba! Darse prisa! Darse prisa!*'

I glanced at the pet. She was holding her hand in front of her mouth as though trying not to laugh.

The beautiful man across from me smiled thinly, and without looking, he reached back and grabbed the waiter's towel as it flicked behind his shoulder. The frenzied server stopped in his tracks, shocked by the arresting hand, his face red around his panting mouth. '*Senor, darse prisa!*' he repeated urgently. '*Darse prisa!*'

My new acquaintance held on to the towel and hauled the waiter in like a gasping mullet. He tipped his head back and spoke softly. 'We do not want to leave,' he said. 'This bomb that terrifies you so much does not worry us. *You* may leave, and you may get everyone else to leave, but we will sit here until I decide otherwise.'

The waiter opened his mouth as if to argue, but no words came out. When he was released he hesitated a moment, then he turned and began urging the rest of the customers out of their seats with maniacal efficiency. In seconds the cafe was empty and silent. I could almost hear the ticking of the bomb and imagine the explosion flinging tables into the air and throwing our bodies around like chaff.

5

'See how they run,' my handsome friend said disdainfully. 'See how they fly from their hive like bees afraid of smoke? See how they scatter in a panic from the scent of impending doom? And yet they do not even see smoke and there is nothing for them to smell. There is no smoke, but they have been smoked out.' He threw his head back and laughed. 'Smoked out by their fear like panicking bees buzzing from their lair.' With a swift, excited movement of his head, he looked at me again. 'Do you like my little joke, Syra? Did you enjoy the spectacle of fear I have arranged especially for you?'

I looked at him, utterly confused.

'Oh, my poor Syra, does it worry you? Do you think a bomb might blow us up at any second? Are you in fear of your life? Do not be afraid, Syra, it is only a hoax.'

'How do you know that?' I asked breathlessly.

'Because it is *my* hoax, *my* little experiment. I wanted to see fear around me and I wanted to treat you to the spectacle.'

'But you didn't know I...'

His melodic laughter cut me off as he stretched his arm over the table. 'Give me your hand, Syra.'

I knew then that I should get up and go. I sensed I was in the presence of danger and knew I should not reach out and touch him. That was my fatal mistake. After that, there was no going back.

He held the tip of one of my fingers between his thumb and forefinger. It was the same finger I had been using less than an hour before to probe my pussy. He held it up, looked at it, and then rested it close to his nostrils. He inhaled the scent of my skin and smiled knowingly. Then he turned my hand, held my finger to his mouth and licked it lightly with his tongue. I could not believe what was happening. His tongue felt warm and wet, and as it ran over the tip of my finger it set my whole body on fire.

The pet giggled, a sort of throaty laugh that scarcely touched her lips, and I sensed her squirming and rubbing her buttocks against the metal seat. Then I felt her pushing the side of one of her feet against the front of my calf. For a second I tried to imagine it was a poodle pressing against me, but the image did not last and I could not resist the excitement growing inside me. This man, this stranger, licked my finger again, tasting the musky scent of my sex and further fanning the flames sweeping through me and burning away my self-control. I edged my leg forward slightly, wondering if she would pull away or if she would return the increased pressure. She pressed harder, and eased herself lower in her chair to slide her leg against mine. I imagined her tight skirt riding up her thighs as they parted just far enough to enclose both my trembling knees.

Suddenly, I heard a man's voice shouting in Spanish. It sounded as though he was barking orders through a megaphone. The crackling electric sound reminded me of my fear and my stomach turned over anxiously.

The beautiful man sitting before me licked my finger again and then slid it into his mouth. I felt the end of it running along the middle of his tongue and the warm saliva pooled there spreading across my knuckle. As he sucked on my

6

digit I felt the blood throbbing at its end like an engorged cock, and as he pulled it slowly out from between his lips, I saw it glistening as though semen was running in a stream down its entire length. He held it in front of his eyes and looked at it closely. I saw how rigid it had become and for a second I felt embarrassed, but I did not relax it.

I heard the pet's high-heels click against the flagstones as she kicked them off, and then I felt the inside of her foot caressing the side of my calf. Excitement spread up my leg and flooded my stomach. I felt her toes clawing against the sensitised skin of my leg, and they seemed to crawl like probing fingers up to my knees. I felt the softness of the underside of her foot as it curled across my knee and continued up to my thigh. I imagined her own thighs spread wide and the edges of her pussy open as she stretched her foot forward, and I felt myself gaping breathlessly as I sensed her creeping, wriggling toes pushing between the soft lips of my sex.

Again I heard the voice shouting through the megaphone. It sounded far away, as though it was coming from a distant horizon, yet its harshness brought back my sense of danger, thrilling me with a shock of fear and deliciously hardening my nipples.

'Syra,' the beautiful man said as he finally loosed his grip on my wet finger, 'can you imagine what it is like to be overcome with sexual excitement and yet at the same time be isolated from the world? Can you imagine the thrill of being penetrated without penetration? Can you picture the warmth of your lover's caress without feeling his arms about you? Can you imagine what it feels like to squeeze your buttocks around a big hard throbbing cock inside you and yet not have your legs wrapped around your lover's hips? Can you imagine the heat of a spanking on your buttocks even before the punishing hand comes down? Can you feel yourself squirming from the stinging blow even before you sense the draft of wind preceding it? Yes, I can see in your eyes that you can. You *can*. I knew it. But although you have imagined it, and now I *know* you have, you have never done it, have you, my dear? You have never experienced that exquisite feeling of detachment at the moment of your highest ecstasy. You do not need to tell me. I can see it in your eyes. You have not done it, have you?'

I wanted to tell him he was right, but I could not speak.

'Would you like me to help you?' he asked gently. 'Would you like me to expose you to your own fears, to allow you to feel the excitement of danger as it seeks out your ecstasy? Would you like me to immunise you from your physical limits and release in you all the sensuality the world has to offer?'

It was as though he knew my thoughts, as though he tapped into the roots of my deepest, darkest desires. It was as though he knew me completely, as though in those few minutes he studied me like a scientist does an insect under a magnifying glass and knew every part of me. 'Yes,' I answered weakly, foolishly, fatally.

'But you must be sure, dear Syra. You must choose whether to come with me or to stay here. My experiment will not work unless you are a volunteer. If you want to be safe you may get up and leave now, but if you want to explore

7

yourself to the limit, if you want to test your desires against your fears, then you must come with me.'

I looked at him uncertainly.

'I could put it like this, my pet. Do you want to be safe or do you want to be bad?'

I knew what I should have done, but I no longer really had a choice. There was something about the way he said *bad* that sounded infinitely better than *safe*, as though *bad* could fill my life completely whereas *safe* meant nothing. I could see he knew what I was thinking. I wanted to say the word just to feel the jolt of fear as it issued from my lips. 'Bad,' I said, 'I want to be bad.'

He sat back in his chair, smiling. 'Oh Syra, do you think I am taken in by your simplicity. You really are *too* obvious. It is almost ridiculous.' He leaned forward again as I felt the pet's toes clawing against the fabric of my panties. 'Syra, my dear, you will have to be more convincing than that. Just saying it is not enough. You have to prove it, and when I am sure you really mean it, then I might take you seriously. When you have shown me you are sincere and you are truly ready to discover yourself, I will give you the chance to search out your limits. You will then be at the point of no return, incapable of finding your way back. Now tell me again, Syra, and this time convince me, do you really want to find out what being truly bad is?'

The pet's toes prized at the edges of my panties. I felt the sharpness of her nails scratching the thin material, and then one of them grazed the soft flesh of my pussy. For a moment I wanted to pull back, but instead I opened my legs slightly and pushed my hips towards her probing toes. The edge of the thin material of my panties cut into my throbbing cunt and parted my outer labia. Her toe followed, slipping between my sex lips, and I slumped even lower in my chair. 'Yes!' I gasped. 'Yes, I want to find out what being truly bad is.'

He pursed his lips and nodded slowly.

I stared at him blankly, not daring to let him see that as the pet's nail scraped across the tip of my clitoris an orgasm began brewing deep within me.

The waiter returned abruptly with two policemen. He pointed, and the officers marched towards us purposefully.

My beautiful new friend smiled at them and got up casually. 'We were just leaving,' he said.

The pet eased her foot back, slipped her shoes on and followed him up.

I struggled to pull the gusset of my panties from between my wet labia, and rose awkwardly.

The two policemen watched Eve intently as she strutted ahead of me, the motion of her tight buttocks urging her short black skirt higher up her thighs. Every seven steps - I counted them - she had to pull it down again with a deft, almost unconscious gesture, pinching the elasticised material between her thumbs and forefingers and smoothing it back down over her hips. I was irritated by her arrogance and her poise, but at the same time I wished she would be distracted by something and forget the routine so I could see higher up between her thighs.

8

I did not know where we were going, where my captor was leading me, all I knew was that I had to follow him.

I must stop writing now. I can hear him turning the key in the lock. He has told me that whenever he comes into the room I must leave what I am writing on the table and sit in the corner until he has read it. I can hardly bear to move with my ankles bound so tightly, so I will have to pull myself across the floor with my hands. I hope I can reach the corner before he comes in or I will be beaten before he even reads my work.

CHAPTER 2

He was here for what felt like ages as I sat silently with my back straight while he perused what I had written. My heart beat hard and fast as he turned the pages, but I kept perfectly still. I have been well trained. He took a red pen and crossed out the word *cunt*. Then he motioned for me to get down in front of him on all fours. I crawled over as well as I could with my ankles bound, and waited with my buttocks thrust up as high as possible, arching my back. I am sure he knew it was not a punishment to beat me - especially not like this with his hand - but he wanted to show me I had done wrong.

I knelt on my hands and knees as he spanked me hard across my naked, upturned buttocks. Each time the flat of his hand came down and the stinging heat of the contact burned my skin, I tightened my cheeks a little more, bringing them together so the insides of my thighs touched and the folds of flesh on each side of my pussy squeezed together. But it was not to withstand the pain that I clenched my bottom, it was to try and contain the joy the spanking gave me, to try and hold back the ecstasy threatening to overtake me. With each hard smack I was driven ever closer to an orgasm that would, when finally released, utterly consume and throw me into a shuddering delirium.

When he finished punishing me I dropped to the floor, exhausted. My pussy was juicing helplessly and I spread my hand across my warm sex to feel the throbbing of my orgasm as it overwhelmed me for a small eternity. I pushed a finger between the fleshy folds of my labia and let the silky wetness run down it onto the base of my hand. I bit my lip as the last jerking pulse faded, and I prayed he would come back soon and punish me again.

For the first time in ages, I slept well. I told myself I had a good night, because of course I do not know what time of day it is. The only night I know is when the candle goes out, and morning comes when he relights it or brings me a fresh one.

We walked for a long time on that hot, bright day on the *Costa del Sol*. I shielded my eyes and saw the pet strutting ahead me, her head held high, her large black sunglasses covering half her face, her long black hair streaming

9

behind her like a horse's tail. I counted her steps, *five, six, seven*, and thought of nothing else. It was as though my whole life was boiled down to her exquisite skirt pulling routine.

We stopped walking on the sandy edge of a small cove. A low harbour wall jutted out into the sea and several small boats bobbed lazily at their moorings. The pet leaned back against a low, whitewashed wall, pulled down her skirt one last time, and began inspecting her fingernails.

I looked at *him*, the man who had led us here. He was staring out at the sea. It was so hot the clear blue water was set on fire by the burning bronze sun. It was as if the world was melting and he was looking serenely out at its demise. His black hair hung straight around his face and he opened his mouth slightly to run his tongue along his dry lips. I felt jealous of that slowly moving tongue; I wanted to use my own to wet his lips, and then I wanted to lie down before him and let him lick my pussy. I wanted to feel the tip of his tongue working its way between the lips of my labia, prising them apart and exposing their inner softness, folding them back as they continued to swell. I wanted him to curl the tip of his tongue around my clitoris, teasing it and drawing it out of its sheath, bringing it out into the open...

He turned and looked at Eve. I realised then I did not know his name, and for a moment I thought of asking him, but it seemed ridiculous, intrusive, too daring.

He looked at me. 'My name is Galen,' he said, as though reading my mind.

I nodded.

He moved towards me and I felt engulfed by the darkness of his haloed shadow. 'It's very hot, Syra,' he stated the obvious. 'Do you feel like taking off your clothes?'

The pet made a quick, bored sighing noise as though she was witnessing something she had seen many times before.

'Is that what people do here?' I asked stupidly.

'Does it matter what people do here?' he retorted mildly.

I shrugged.

'What do *you* want to do, Syra? That is the real question. What do *you* want? Or are you too full of fears to even think about it?'

I felt reprimanded by his mocking tone and exposed by it, as though he could see behind my eyes to my soul. I looked at the pet, but all her attention was still on her fingernails. 'Maybe,' I retorted defensively. 'Yes, maybe.'

He laughed again, but this time his tone was gentler when he spoke. 'Oh Syra, you have a long way to go before you even know what being truly bad is.'

I was stung by his comment, and believing he was about to abandon me as hopeless, my stomach clenched anxiously. 'If I want to take my clothes off, then I will,' I said quickly. 'I'll do anything I want to do.'

'But you may not want to do anything, and so you would do nothing,' he countered. '*You* cannot be the measure of your desires, my pet. Your desires may not be worth reaching for.'

'Well, we shall see,' I said petulantly as I undid the top button of my red dress

10

and kicked off both my sandals. The sand was surprisingly hot, and I screwed up my toes to try and protect the soles of my feet.

Galen laughed yet again and turned back towards the sea.

I undid the next button, but I felt spurned. My efforts seemed pointless without him observing me, so I loosened my grip on the third button as I was filled with despondency.

He spun around and stared at me.

Like a machine switched on again, I began undoing my buttons. The last one came free and I parted the front of my dress so my cleavage was fully visible.

'Eve,' he said abruptly, 'show my new little pet how to respond properly.'

The pet looked up and smiled. She walked over to stand in front of him, and then pulled her skirt down so the hem was at the proper place halfway down her slender thighs. 'What do you want me to do, Galen?' she enquired.

'Strip,' he replied curtly.

She crossed her hands, grabbed the bottom edge of her thin white shirt, and pulled it up over her head. She lifted it high and her well-formed breasts rose tautly, their rounded sides curving beautifully against her chest, complementing the sculpted hollows of her closely shaved armpits and leading delectably to her hard pink nipples. She closed her eyes for a moment as she looked up into the sun through her black sunglasses and dropped her shirt to the sand. Then she gripped the waist of her tight skirt and began pushing it down, slowly. The waistband stretched as it moved away from her slim waist and followed the shape of her hips. She did not wriggle, but expanded the material to its limit against her buttocks as she forced it down over her thighs. When she let it go it fell around her ankles and she stepped out of it, kicking her sandals off at the same time. She stood in the bright light with a black thong pulled up tightly against her fleshy pudenda, the sun's rays reflecting on the black panes of her sunglasses. She ran the underside of one of her thumbs against the thin waistband of the thong, pulled it away from her skin, and holding the thin triangle of material at its front, drew it down to just above her knees. Then she simply stood there for a moment as though arrested by the fact of her own nakedness, as if exposing her carefully trimmed black pubic hair was simply too tantalising, too exciting to bear, then she bent her knees inward, and letting go of the thong, let it fall to the sand. Now she stood completely naked staring out at the blinding sea. 'Galen?' she asked, sounding strangely lost.

He did not need a fully formed question from her; he could see the craving in her eyes even through the dark shades protecting them. 'Bend over, my pet,' he instructed her. 'Stretch your arms out and place your hands against the wall and remain still. I want Syra to watch how you obey. It will be her first lesson.' He turned back towards me. 'Come closer, Syra, my pet. I want you to see what it is to be bad.'

I went and stood near to him, trembling.

Eve leaned forward, bending at the waist as she stretched her arms out and placed her hands against the white stone wall. Her shoulders were strong, the muscles and tendons running across them well defined. Her back was slim and

11

elegant, lightly tanned and narrowing deliciously into her waist. Fresh red stripes ran at an angle from the top of her right arm to below her left shoulder blade. Bent forward, her buttocks were even tighter and their firm curves were accentuated by the slight strain of her position. Several more red lines ran across her bottom cheeks. She placed her legs slightly apart and I glimpsed in the darkness at the tops of her thighs a fine wisp of pubic hair.

I stood by Galen but could not take my eyes off Eve. She remained perfectly still; I could hardly see her breathing. It was as though she was in a trance, unable to move and strangely immune from the forces controlling the physical world. I watched a tiny bead of perspiration form between her shoulder blades and run slowly down the perfect indentation in the centre of her back. For a moment I worried Galen would see it and disapprove as it flowed like a tear between her buttocks. Still she did not move, and another tear of perspiration formed on her back and began its journey down over the thin red stripes left behind by her last punishment.

'Galen,' I said, 'I don't like this. Can we go now, I...'

He put a finger to his lips and silenced me. 'Quiet, my pet, there is someone coming. Don't you want to learn? Have you forgotten so soon that this is a lesson? Surely you do not want to run away even before the instruction begins?'

I looked back at the pet as a man stepped around the corner of the wall. He was dark and swarthy, with an unshaven face and dirty clothes. He stopped when he saw Eve stretched motionless before the wall.

'Do you like what you see?' Galen asked him.

The man seemed unsure of what to do or say, but finally he nodded slowly. 'Si, senor.'

'Would you like to fuck her?'

The stranger looked surprised. He glanced at me, nodding, and I flushed red with embarrassment. 'Si, senor, I would like to fuck her.'

'Good, but do not expect her to move. I have decided she will remain still. Do you understand?'

The man eagerly nodded again.

'And I want my new pet, Syra, to watch. I want her to know what being truly bad is.'

The stranger sniggered and stood directly behind Eve. He ran a large, rough hand across the red strips marking her shoulders as if expecting her to respond to his touch, but she remained absolutely still. He glanced back at me again, and smiled lasciviously as he ran his finger down the shallow valley of her back. The drop of perspiration making its way down towards her buttocks absorbed the dirt from his fingertip and left an oily smear down her spine that glistened in the hot sun.

I could hardly bear to watch, but somehow I could not stop myself. I looked around, wondering if there was anyone else who could see. Some young men were playing with a ball near the edge of the sea. One of them turned around and waved at me when he noticed me looking at him, but I dropped my head shyly and ignored him.

12

The swarthy man pulled up tightly behind Eve and quickly undid the front of his trousers. He took out his swelling cock and pressed its thick tip between her bottom cheeks. I waited for her to move, but she did not. She was doing exactly as she had been ordered to do and remaining utterly motionless. Galen smiled at me, but I could not smile back. I was too nervous and too excited. I watched as the man bent his legs slightly and levelled his now fully erect penis at the base of Eve's buttocks, circling slowly until he found the soft entrance to her vagina. Then he straightened his legs and pushed his cock up inside her until I could no longer see any of it. At first he held her around the waist, but as he began thrusting he grabbed her by the hips to brace himself. He left oily smears on her skin where he gripped her, and as his dark face reddened, he bent his legs at the knees again and moved his hips back and forth frantically. He reached around and grabbed her breasts, squeezing them roughly and pinching her nipples fiercely between his fingertips, but even though she must have been in pain, she still did not move a muscle. He bent his head to bite her shoulder and drove violently into her, groaning and gripping her hair like a horse's mane as he climaxed deep inside her, riding her fiercely while she showed no more feeling than a beautiful statue.

After his orgasm ebbed, the man pulled out of Eve and stood for a moment with semen glistening on the tip of his penis. Then, as if suddenly reminded of something vital, he hurriedly zipped up his trousers.

Galen smiled at him and tossed some *pesetas* onto the ground.

The stranger bent over to pick them up, and without a second glance at Eve, scurried off.

Galen put the palms of his hands on my cheeks and turned my face towards the young men still playing on the beach. 'Would you like me to invite them up as well, Syra?' he asked me quietly.

His hands felt cool on my hot face, and as I dropped my head, I felt warm moisture dampening the thin fabric of my panties. My legs felt weak and I gasped as though his mere touch threatened to bring on an orgasm. I sensed a nervous tug in the depths of my belly and my nipples were hard against my dress. Almost without realising what I was doing, I pressed a hand down between my thighs as I continued watching the young men playing on the beach, even after Galen let go of my face. The one who had waved at me abandoned the game to move closer and stare at me. I pressed my lips together and dropped my eyes, feeling totally ashamed.

'Oh Syra,' Galen sighed. 'You have no idea of what being bad is, have you?'

I could have run away right there and then. I could have run away from him and the future he was creating for me, but his words seemed to challenge me, to stop me and hold me back. I wanted to stamp my foot and show him what was happening to me. I wanted to scream in frustration and throw myself at his feet. I wanted to lick his black leather shoes and wait until he told me what to do.

'But do you still want to find out, Syra?'

'Yes,' I said without hesitation.

'Shall I test you?'

'Yes,' I insisted like a stupid fawn asking to be devoured by a wolf.

He turned to the pet. 'I release you, Eve,' he said firmly. 'Come. Get dressed. We have things to do. We have to test a new pet.'

Eve shivered as if just awakening from a sorcerer's spell. She looked at me over the top of her sunglasses as she bent to retrieve her thong. It was covered in sand, but she pulled it up against her semen-smeared pussy without shaking it clean. She unbuttoned her shirt before putting it back on, and as she slowly did up the buttons, I detected a jealous gleam in her eyes even through her sunglasses, as if she knew I was important to Galen and resented it. She puckered her lips and sneered at me as she slipped on her skirt and picked up her sandals. Galen was already holding my hand and dragging me towards the road as she ran along behind us, struggling to put on her shoes. I knew she wanted to shout for him to wait, and at the same time I knew she had long since realised he would never wait for anyone.

He haled a taxi, and we all climbed in. He leaned forward over the front seat and in Spanish gave instructions to the driver, a slim, dark-haired youth who laughed and said something back.

'No,' Galen replied in English as he stared at me, 'she does not know yet where she is going, but I'm sure she will enjoy it.'

The driver laughed again throatily, obviously in on the secret.

I did not know where we were going, that much was true, and I wonder if I would have gone so willingly had I known. None of us know what lies before of us or how the future is connected to the present. It is ridiculous to think we can avoid things, for every event connects to another. How could I have guessed that taxi ride would ultimately lead me to this place in which I am now imprisoned?

CHAPTER 3

During what I call night, he came and pulled the door open slightly. He stood watching me silently, in front of a shaft of light silhouetting him. I had not been able to sleep even though I was exhausted, and as soon as I saw him there, I picked up a pencil and started scribbling frantically. I did not want him to think I was slacking, and I kept writing until he finally pushed the door closed again, bolted it and left. Most of what I wrote was mere fantasy - my wishes and desires - so I have thrown it into the rubbish pile. Every time he comes, he inspects this pile to make sure I have not thrown anything away which is important.

I sat between Galen and the pet in the back of the hot cab. Eve kept squirming her hips and shoving against me as if I was a cuckoo invading her nest. I pushed back once, and she dug one of her sharp fingernails into my arm. It made tears spring to my eyes, but I did not say anything. I stared vacuously through the window as we travelled out of town. Eventually Galen tapped the driver's

14

shoulder and we pulled out onto a dusty track. A stone amphitheatre, its upper walls vertically boarded and topped by a circular veranda, loomed directly ahead of us.

'*La plaza de toros, senor*,' the driver announced, as he turned in his seat and held his hand out for payment. He stared at my knees as he waited for Galen to produce the cash, and I opened them slightly so he could see as far as my panties. He licked his lips, and I opened my legs a little more.

It was late afternoon, and although the sun was lower in the sky the heat still hit me like a wall of fire as we emerged from the cab. I shielded my eyes from the brightness and looked around me. The arena dominated a collection of squat white houses with red roofs. It stood isolated on a shallow crest in the undulating, scrub-covered Andalusian countryside, and I was startled by a sudden roar from within it, a deep, bloodthirsty sound followed by a unified screech of joy and fear clearly generated by people observing someone else's suffering. The sound made me shiver, and for a moment in the blazing sunlight I felt cold, as though the screaming crowd had blasted me with an icy gale.

Galen led the way into the dark entrance tunnel at the base of the bullring. He bought tickets at a small kiosk, and a few paces further on we emerged onto the packed lower terraces. It was so hot it was like standing in hell. There was another sudden, bloodcurdling roar from the crowd as a group of brightly dressed men walked out into the arena in a neat procession. Everyone around us jumped to their feet and started clapping, shouting and cheering. Galen led us halfway around the stadium, until we were in the shade, and we were shown to seats halfway up the banked staging. I flopped down onto the bench and fanned myself with a programme as Galen sat on one side of me and Eve perched on the other.

'The bulls have already been allocated,' he informed me, leaning against me but not taking his eyes from the procession of men. 'I do not recognise the third matador, but look, Espartaco is here, at the head of the procession, and so is Uceda Litri. The crowd will expect much from Espartaco in such company.'

He had become completely immersed in what was going on, and I could hardly believe that less than an hour ago he was paying a stranger to have sex with Eve on a public beach. I looked at her. She was staring straight ahead and pressing her lips together to moisten them. They glistened invitingly, and I suffered an urge to lick them and taste their sweetness.

Espartaco stood proudly with his assistants surrounding him, his suit shining brilliantly with red, green and gold sequins. His companions' outfits were less rich but no less dazzling, their silver and purple more humbly reflecting his ostentatious radiance. A white shirt, a narrow black tie, a green sash knotted at his waist, pink knee-high stockings, black slippers and a black two-cornered hat completed Espartaco's fabulous costume. As he bowed to the crowd, he drew his hat down and let it almost scrape the ground. Bending low, he exposed a small pigtail clipped with a gold buckle at the back of his head. His muscular thighs bulged inside his tight trousers, and the clingy stretch material outlined his tight bottom. He stood up straight again and thrust his hips forward to accentuate the bulging outline of his cock, then he drew his cape from his shoulders and strutted around the arena, swirling it towards the spectators and making them whoop with excitement. Finally, he stood immediately below where we sat, looked up at Galen and swung the soft black cape back across his shoulder.

Galen nodded to him and the crowd cheered wildly. I glanced down shyly as everyone clapped and looked admiringly at my captor. He stood up and acknowledged first Espartaco's tribute and then the admiration of the people. I felt like a handmaiden to a Roman emperor and shivered with excitement, both at what was actually happening and what was taking place in my mind. Two rows above us was a specially built box jutting out from the line of terraced seats, curtained ostentatiously with red velvet. A man stood up and leaned forward over the front edge of the box, holding his arms high. He was in his mid-forties with jet-black hair and a square, tanned face. He wore a dark suit, and over his jacket ran two light-blue ribbons draped over each of his shoulders and crossing at his chest.

'The president,' Galen informed me. 'He will order the first bull to be released.'

The president gave a signal, a fanfare of trumpets sounded, and a young black tightly muscled bull galloped into the ring. He snorted and turned in all directions as the matador's assistants tested him with large purple capes.

'And now we will see how our first young combatant performs,' Galen whispered to me.

Eve started studying her long fingernails again. 'Galen,' she said in a whining tone, leaning across me as if I was not even there. 'Galen, I'm bored. Can't we do something more exciting?'

'No,' he said firmly.

'But it's so hot and I'm so thirsty,' she complained.

He ignored her.

She waved to a man selling drinks from a small tray, but he did not see her. She pouted and stood up, pushing past the people seated alongside her. Adjusting her skirt in the usual way every seven steps, she made her way down the open stairway between the rows of seats. I watched her progress, deliberate and purposeful, amid the pent-up excitement of the noisy crowd. I felt envious of her confidence as she took a drink from the man's tray, and then pointed to Galen as the one responsible for paying for it. The vendor nodded, but then walked in the opposite direction as though the idea of pursuing the debt made him uncomfortable. She drove a thick straw into the container, closed her full lips around its end, tightened her cheeks, and sucked enthusiastically. The red liquid flowed up the translucent straw, and I saw the movement of her throat as she swallowed it. She took the straw deeper into her mouth, sucking harder, and I imagined the cool liquid spurting against the back of her throat. As I watched, her regular swallowing became a continuous feeding, then I saw her cheeks relax as her lips, slowly and begrudgingly, released the thick straw. A sparkling drop of liquid fell from her chin as she licked her lips and gazed up at the sun with an intense look of satisfaction.

There was a sudden roaring cheer as the picadors entered the ring. Their

16

horses, swathed in thick protective quilts, snorted and dipped their heads as the riders lowered their lances at the still vigorous bull. Hooves scooped up puffs of red dust and the hot air was thick with the smell of sand and sweat and with the clamour of excitement heralding a public execution.

I did not watch the first death. I looked down at my feet as the crowd roared and the exhausted animal snorted its last painful breaths. The second kill I did not see either, but this time I stared at the victim until the last moment and only closed my eyes as the young *banderillero* leapt in front of the stricken bull and drove the barbed, colourfully decorated stick into the nape of the animal's blood-streaked neck. But when Espartaco entered the ring and Galen leapt to his feet and the crowd broke out into uncontrollable howling, I could not look away. The bullfighter's suit shone more brightly now as the rays of the setting sun picked out every dazzling facet of his exquisitely sequined jacket. The picadors backed away from the bull and Espartaco walked across the arena to stand beneath us. He bowed again to Galen, and when Galen lifted his hands high and clapped them once, the crowd went wild.

Espartaco turned to the bull, already exhausted and running with blood from wounds caused by the shiny, silver-tipped lances of the picadors. The beautiful animal bent its front legs and almost knelt on the dusty ground as it prepared to charge. Espartaco walked towards it slowly, his cape hanging loosely from his right arm. He stood in front of his victim, and passed his cape to his other hand. The bull looked enraged, but seemed incapable of movement, as though he was transfixed by the glittering figure before him. The crowd shouted angrily, annoyed at the bull for not responding to Espartaco, for being too easily seduced by its master, for not fighting, for not showing its will to live. But the outrage of the spectators could not put courage into the poor beast's heart. Finally, Espartaco turned his back on it and looked up at the crowd in exasperation. There was nothing for him to do. He was prepared to battle for his life, but his chosen opponent was not brave enough to take him on. He dropped his cape by his side, and denied the contest along with the chance to romance his worshippers, he threw a single, petulant kiss at them, bowed once more to Galen, and walked out of the arena without looking back.

The president ordered a fanfare of trumpets, but it did not drown out the jeering outrage of the crowd as the cowardly bull was knocked down, bound around the ankles and dragged away by its feet. The stadium was filled with frustrated anger, and the spectators' growing indignation combined with physical discomfort was an explosive combination. I felt as if I were drowning in a boiling cauldron of rage. Galen pulled me along the aisle and up the staging towards the president's box. The president was holding his head in his hands, and Galen dragged me along by the wrist until I was standing anxiously in front of the forlorn figure.

'Syra, my pet, meet Senor Vincente de Mora, the president of our famous bullfight.'

The president looked up and his dark eyes fell directly on me, but he did not seem to see me. He was consumed by his own despair as he stared straight ahead, his turned down lips almost snarling and his thick, black eyebrows furrowed with anger and embarrassment. He opened his mouth as if to speak, but then dropped his face abruptly into his hands again.

'My dear Mora, do not be so unhappy,' Galen implored him. 'Look, I have a new pet and she is determined to show me how devoted she is to the thought of fulfilling all her desires by conquering all her fears.'

Mora lifted his face from his hands again, and raised an eyebrow. 'Syra?' he said thoughtfully, as if slowly recovering from his melancholy. 'A pretty thing... yes, very pretty.'

His accent was strong and I sensed a cruel note in his voice. He struck me as a man who claimed his own pleasures above everyone else's. I did not like him and I wanted to leave. I pulled against Galen's grip, but my weak struggle only amused him.

'Look, Mora, my little pet is trying to escape. I think you have frightened her, like Espartaco frightened his bull.'

The president of the bullfight laughed mockingly.

Galen turned to me. 'Do not be afraid, my little pet. Remember, you are only here because you choose to be, not like the poor bull who failed so sadly to reward us all with a good fight and a courageous death.'

'Do not remind me,' Mora said angrily. 'I wish to forget it! Perhaps your Syra can distract me?'

'Can you?' Galen asked me, looking deeply into my eyes.

I felt like looking away, so I looked at Mora. It was the wrong thing to do, for straightaway I realised he did not like my direct regard.

'She looks as if she is challenging me, my dear Galen, and I do not like that.' His heavily accented voice was cold and deliberate. I sensed anger in him and stared down at my feet, kicking at a discarded plastic cup.

'Test her, then,' Galen urged. 'She wants it. That is why she is here with me. She says she wants to discover how to be truly bad. See if you can help her find the wickedness she craves.'

I looked up at him from lowered lids as Mora tightened his mouth and nodded thoughtfully. His interest was caught; I felt the cold edge of his curiosity like a blade poised over my heart. 'She is a fidget, though,' he complained. 'Look, she cannot stand still even though she knows we are talking about her.'

'Then that would be a good test, don't you think, seeing if she can stand still?'

The president nodded slowly as he rose and walked around me, eyeing me up and down like a slave in a market. 'Yes, my dear Galen, you are, as always, right. It would be a good test, indeed. Come Syra, stand here at the front of the presidential box, look out over the arena, and show yourself to the crowd.'

Obediently, I moved to the front edge of the small box and rested my hands on the ornamental iron balustrade. I felt people's eyes on me at once wondering who I was, and stiffening my arms, I leaned further out.

Mora stepped up behind me, and despite how hot the day was I could still feel the distinct heat of his body. Then I felt his scorching breath on my neck as he bent his face to my ear.

18

'Do not move, Syra,' he said quietly. 'Stay still. I do not want you to move. You must remain where you are, standing in front of the crowd, exactly as you are now... yes, Syra, that is it, completely motionless until I tell you otherwise. You may breathe, of course, but I do not want to see your chest moving, and you may not move your eyes at all. I want you to stare at your subjects no matter what happens.'

I was already staring into the crowd and did not alter my line of sight. I breathed shallowly and hoped he would not be able to detect the slight rise and fall of my breasts. I felt his hands alight on my hips and very gently push my dress up, exposing the naked flesh below the edge of my panties. The act of remaining perfectly still multiplied the thrills beginning to course through me. I wanted to be uncovered, exposed, shown off to the crowd. I wanted him to lift my dress all the way up over my breasts and pull my panties down. I wanted him to reveal my pussy to everyone, to expose the soft pink flesh of my labia, and I wanted him to shove his knee between my legs and open them wide so everyone could see my most private parts. The crowd suddenly roared again and I felt him pulling down the front of my panties. Holding my dress up around my hips with one hand, he tugged hard on my panties with the other and brought them down around my knees.

I wanted to squirm and press my pussy against his hard palm, but I was not allowed to move. I did not even grip the balustrade any tighter, even though I was desperate to relieve some of the tension building up inside me like floodwater behind a dam. I watched the crowd impassively, my mind racing, my stomach churning with excitement and my mind ablaze with images igniting my every nerve ending with lust. I saw the men in the crowd ogling my exposed vulva, some of them licking their lips with anticipation and some pulling their cocks out of their trousers to cradle them in their hands, rubbing them as the sight of my exposed pussy drove them on. I waited, with every second sinking deeper into an ecstatic oblivion beyond all physical expression, affording no outlet and no bounds.

Mora lifted the front of my dress all the way up and held it just below my chin, exposing my breasts as he wedged his arm between them. I felt the palm of his right hand pressing across the flesh of my buttocks, and then his finger slipping into their tight valley. Its tip glanced across the soft edges of my labia, and the wet petals opened for him like a ripe fig. I stared at the crowd without moving, and as they roared again, he removed his hand. There was a moment's pause - a brief, silent eternity - then his hand came down on my bottom with a shocking smack. I was not sure if my buttocks tightened inadvertently beneath the impact. I hoped they did not. I wanted to please Galen, to do as he had commanded, but I was not sure I could. My cheeks burned hot and my chest tightened. The president lifted his hand, and brought it down again even harder across my bottom. The sharp slapping sound was almost drowned out by the cries of the crowd, and I was sure my muscles tensed and I swallowed harder than I should have. Then a third blow fell and I felt my teeth grinding together, holding back my need to cry out.

19

I felt something sharp against my side, and out of the corner of my eye saw another figure standing close behind me, but I could not tell who it was. Then I smelled her strong, citrus-like perfume, and the sharp touch turned agonising as Eve dug her fingernails deep into my waist. For a second I was able to resist the pain, which harmonised with the humiliation of my exposure, complemented my captivity and mysteriously heightened my arousal, but the moment passed, and as Mora's hand came down for a fourth blow I cried out, I could not help myself. As I heard myself wail in distress I knew I had failed, and the ecstasy building up inside me subsided, replaced by a sinking disappointment and a sobering flood of self-disgust.

I heard Mora laugh mockingly. 'She has failed, Galen. What do you do when someone fails in what is expected of them?'

'They have to be trained more rigorously, my dear Mora,' came the cool reply.

It was as though their voices were reaching me from a distant horizon; they sounded far away and strangely hollow, almost disembodied, but like the sirens' song, they were also strangely irresistible. For a while I continued to hold on to the balustrade, trying to convince Mora I'd succeeded, that somehow my regained quietness and rigidity proved I was being completely obedient. But I knew I had failed. I had allowed the pet to destroy my chance to prove myself. I turned to Galen in the hope of seeing him smile or nod at me understandingly, but his arm was around Eve's shoulder and he was talking quietly into her ear, ignoring me.

I am going to stop writing now because I can hear him coming. His footsteps ring on the cold stone floor, and the way he rattles the keys makes me horribly anxious. I ought to be used to it by now, but I wonder if I ever will be. I hope I have gotten enough done to please him, but I suspect I have not. Somehow I think he would have wanted me to produce more by now.

CHAPTER 4

He has gone. He spent a long time going through what I had written. He didn't say anything, but he looked up at me a couple of times to make sure I was sitting correctly - upright, with my back stiff, my mouth closed, my eyes looking straight ahead. Sometimes it reminds me of when I had the chopsticks bound together at right angles across my mouth, pinioning my lips together and forcing them outwards like a bill. Usually he does not like me blinking, either, yet occasionally, if he thinks I have done well, he allows me to as a sort of treat. This time he seemed in such a bad mood I knew there would be no favours, so I just stared straight ahead. For a while I thought of what it had been like to feel pain. It came back to me vaguely, that exquisite feeling of surrendering to punishment, and even as I thought about it I was aware of the aching in my shoulders as my muscles strained to keep me from moving. Staring without blinking for so long has also made my eyes sore, and that is another good sign.

20

Perhaps it means I'm getting better...

He left another pencil for me, but no food. I was hungry, but I could tell from the way he looked at me when he left that I was to get no food until I had done more work. I know he is displeased with what I've written so far, but I can do nothing except tell the truth. That is what he told me to do, and that is what I am doing, I think.

Yet it did not stop him from beating me again. He spanked me hard before he left. This time he made me lie on my back and lifted my bound ankles high, until the base of my back was lifted clear off the floor. The outer flesh of my pussy was squeezed tightly shut, and I knew when his hand came down it would catch my vulva as well as the tightly stretched cheeks of my bottom.

The first three smacks I hardly felt - it was as though the flat of his hand was a caress, a warmly welcomed kiss, the glancing touch of a tender lover - but the next three blows were harder, and I winced each time I felt the smarting sting as his palm smacked loudly against my skin.

The smacks that followed were even harder to endure on my flaming flesh, and my labia prickled with heat as I felt it go from a soft pink to a bright red. As each slap landed I spun on my suspended ankles, twisting and turning, engrossed in the agonising pleasure, utterly absorbed in the torment.

It finally ended as he let my legs drop to the floor. I moaned, and as I lay with my bound legs splayed open at the knees, he smacked his hand across my exposed pussy one last time and drove three fingers deep inside me. His digits were warm and hard and my sex lips were so sore that scarcely had the knuckles of his hand parted my pussy when I climaxed with a heavy, jerking convulsion.

But I must get on now. There is so much to write down and so much to remember and I must not make any mistakes...

We all sat down at the table in the president's box. It was constructed from exquisitely worked iron, its heavy feet splayed into large, talon-like claws, each of the four legs ornamented with an ascending spiral of rampaging bulls with flaring nostrils. A heavy red cloth - the same material as the curtains draped around the edges of the box - was spread across the table, which was laid out with glasses, several open bottles of red wine and small silver dishes containing a variety of nuts and olives. Galen and Mora sat with their backs to the bullring while I sat facing them. The pet leaned lazily against the side of the box staring into the crowd, occasionally biting one of her long nails or tipping her sunglasses back up from the bridge of her nose as she observed the people shifting restlessly in their seats.

Mora poured wine and he and Galen sat back and stared at me, glasses in hand, making me feel rather like a mannequin in a shop window, only they were considering whether or not they wanted *me*, not the clothes I was wearing.

'Will Espartaco come out again?' Galen asked, not taking his dark eyes off my face.

'Yes, oh yes,' Mora replied as he sipped his wine. 'The crowd has not taken well to the poor display of our last competitor. They will have to find another challenger for the great Espartaco or we will have a riot.'

'I hope it will be an *approved* challenger and no less.'

'Of course, my dear man, of course.'

Galen smiled and drained his glass. 'I hope so. We cannot have the fearless Espartaco facing a truly brave bull, now can we?'

'Do not worry, but allow the crowd a bit of a show. It is a bullring, after all.'

They both laughed as Mora refilled their glasses.

'But what about my new pet?' Galen asked. 'I cannot say *she* is in any way approved yet.'

'I am disappointed.' Mora sighed dramatically. 'I thought you were an expert in such matters. I am very disappointed, indeed.'

'I have not had time to bring her on yet. You must understand she is still fresh and untrained.'

I looked down, embarrassed. It felt strange the way they were talking about me as though I was not there or as if I was a mere object who could not understand them. I felt ashamed and disgusted with myself. I had let Galen down and made myself look stupid. I had been so sure the test he set me would be easy, and my arrogance had made me look ridiculous. He held a bottle above an empty glass, looked at me and raised his eyebrows. I nodded, desperate for a drink, and he filled the glass to the brim.

'Try not to spill it, Syra,' he said wryly.

I reached out and took the glass nervously. I could barely stop my hands from shaking, and I lifted it to my lips quickly in case some wine should spill over the edge. It tasted rich and warm, and even as I swallowed it I felt the alcohol's dizzying effect. The heat in the arena was intense, billowing up from the lower levels and curling around us like a dragon's invisible breath. I felt beads of perspiration breaking out on my forehead and my heart started pounding.

'Well, at least she can do *something* properly,' Mora observed sarcastically.

'I think we should give her another chance,' Galen suggested magnanimously. 'What do you think, Syra my pet, do you deserve another chance?'

I was not sure whether I should reply. Something inside me was telling me to get up and walk away, to toss my head back indignantly and leave them to their silly games. 'Yes,' I said in a pitifully small voice, 'please.'

'You see.' Galen smiled. 'She is not yet a lost cause.'

Below us the crowd let out a huge, booming roar.

'Ah, and so it begins again.' Mora placed the bottle down hard on the table and leaned an arm back over the curtained front of the box.

There was another great roar from the spectators and a wave of sticky heat billowed up from beneath us. Eve leaned sideways against the balustrade, her hipbones pushing out sharply against her thin skirt as it curved over her buttocks, taking their shape. She caressed her hair back and rubbed her slender neck, turning her head in a circle as though easing some tension in her upper back. She thrust out the tip of her tongue and ran its glossy redness first along her top lip and then along her bottom lip. As she did so her mouth glistened in the sun, which was beginning to pour over the edges of the box. I felt an

22

overwhelming wave of desire for her. I wanted to taste her lips against my own. I wanted to caress her slender neck and feel her long hair falling around my face, her writhing limbs intertwined with mine. I wanted to hear her breathing fast and watch her listening to my own panting gasps. I wanted to straddle her face, wrapping my thighs around her head. I wanted to press my pussy against her mouth as she drove her tongue deep into my wetness. I wanted to revel in the passionate energy of her body in the overbearing heat as I absorbed her scent, molecule by molecule, through the pores of my skin...

'At last it seems they have found one,' Galen declared.

I stood up so I could see. A stocky black bull was running into the ring. He stopped in the centre, his bloodshot eyes ablaze. Stiff-necked, he looked around seeking out threats. He twisted in a pirouette, circling in the air with all his feet off the ground, as a horse charged towards him. The picador, straight- backed and glistening like a jewel in his sequined suit, held the reins high in one hand as with the other he levelled his lance at the creature's throat. The bull pulled away and snorted loudly before charging at the horse and ramming its horns deep into the quilted protection running down its sides. He gored it, deceived into thinking he was gutting the horse; deceived into believing he was already claiming victory.

Eve looked away from the spectacle and picked up a glass from the table. Her long fingernails clinked against it, filling a brief moment of ominous silence, which was broken when the crowd, having drawn a collective breath, roared again. I looked at her, hoping to see a friendly smile at last, but she pursed her full lips slightly and turned her head away contemptuously.

Like Mora, Galen leaned back over the balustrade and stared down into the bullring. 'Aren't you looking, Syra?' he shouted back at me without turning his head. 'Doesn't it excite you? Perhaps you do not know what excites you?' He swung around to face me. 'Syra, my pet, how can you tackle your fears, how can you know when you are acting out your wishes if you do not know what excites you?'

'I *do* know,' I yelled, but the noise of the crowd drowned out my words.

He cupped his hand around one of his ears and cocked his head to one side, raising his eyebrows as if encouraging me to try again. 'What was that you said, Syra?'

'I *do* know...'

'You will have to come closer, my pet. Come closer and tell me.'

I stepped forward, feeling as though I was being invited to slip into bed with my lover. I could feel the heat of anticipation running across my flesh, prickling across my skin and making me shiver. He held up his palm as a signal. Perhaps, like a considerate lover, he wanted me to walk more slowly, to take my time, not to rush. I stopped, and felt myself licking my lips like Eve. I wanted him to see the dazzling reflection of the sun's rays on my mouth. I wanted him to yearn to kiss me.

'No, my pet,' he said, shaking his head.

His tone thrilled me and I licked my lips again to stop them becoming too dry for him.

'No, my pet,' he repeated, 'come to me on your knees.'

I thought at first I had misunderstood him, and I must have looked surprised for he repeated himself.

'On your knees, beneath the table, Syra.'

The shock of his words paralysed me. I understood them, of course, but their stunning import on my mind was part of my humiliation, and I needed a moment's angry indignation or I would not have had anything against which to measure my fall.

The crowd roared even more loudly and Galen looked over the balustrade again. He did not turn back towards me; he would issue no further instructions. Slowly, I bent my legs, placed my hands on the edge of the table and leaned forward. He was not even watching me. He was not even bothered to see if I obeyed his orders. I felt the pressure of the edge of the table against the hot palms of my hands. I felt as if I was clinging to a raft exposed to a stormy sea, not knowing if I would drown or survive. I did not know whether or not to sink below the table as if deliberately falling into hell, or whether to pull myself back, sit down and carry on as if nothing had happened. I gripped the edge of the table more tightly and bent my legs a little more. Still he did not look at me, but in the corner of my eye I glimpsed Eve's disdainful glance and it was enough to spur me on.

I hardly know how to describe what I felt as I lowered myself below the edge of the table. I was excited and filled with anticipation, but I did not know why I was excited or what I was expecting. More than anything, I was gripped by a sense of profound humiliation. I felt like an animal only doing what it was told. But it was not a simple, straightforward humiliation for it was coupled with the disdain of the man I was allowing to become my master. My degradation was enhanced by his deliberate ignorance of my actions. No matter how much I obeyed him I could not hold his interest, and it was his lack of interest that stubbornly intensified my willingness to obey him and made the humiliation I experienced so delectable and so complete.

As I sank below the surface of the iron table, I felt the heavy warmth of the red cloth against the tip of my nose and its soft caress against my forehead. Then the cloth draped over my eyes and all I could see was a deep red glow, as if the setting sun had descended to the horizon and I was watching it sink with me into a boiling sea of ecstasy. The pleat of heavy red material stroked my face, caressing it. I smelled a deep rich scent of warm velvet evocative of wine and passion. Then, as I lowered myself completely below the table, the cloth slipped away and I felt as though a mysterious blindness had been lifted from me.

I was holding my hands above my head, still gripping the edge of the table. I felt as if I was floating deep within a molten sea. I saw Galen's legs on one side of me and Mora's thicker legs on the other. One of Eve's feet was tapping the floor, her sandal tipping slightly away from the sole of her foot every time she lifted it. I remained squatting for some time, listening to the roar of the crowd and the heavy rumbling that echoed around the terraces as everyone surged to their feet at the same time. I heard a dragon-like hiss as they all sighed in unison, and felt the increased pressure in the air as they thrust their clenched fists high above their heads. It was as though I was plugged into the emotions of everyone there, experiencing every sensation available, as if I suddenly possessed an infinite capacity to absorb feelings and emotions.

I watched Galen's legs, for they were my goal. The tumult of sensations did not die down inside me, but with every impression I absorbed I seemed to develop an even greater capacity for receptivity than was capable of being satisfied. I needed more. I was nowhere near filled. I released my tightly gripping fingers from around the edge of the table and placed the palms of my hands flat on the floor. I shivered as I felt the roughness of the boards. I crouched there for a while, aware of the lines of my body, sensing the curved angle of my back and the way it bloomed up into my hips. I felt my chest tightening as I experienced the taut shape of my upturned buttocks and the sense of exposure that came with it. I kept looking forward at Galen's dark slacks, but I could not move. I waited, and the saddle of my back dropped even lower, causing my bottom to move higher, and I felt the tightness of the gusset of my panties pulling against my sex. My pussy was hot and moist and swollen, and shivering with delight, I arched my back even more deeply to pull the material of my panties as tightly as possible against my sensitive labia.

At last I moved, picking up one of my hands and stretching it forward deliberately. I watched it as though it was someone else's hand, but I knew it was mine as in the moment of contact with the wooden board my body was set on fire in a way that had nothing to do with the heat of the day. I felt my flesh igniting from within as though every one of my nerve endings had been lit at the same time. I moved my other hand, and felt myself edging inexorably towards Galen's legs. It was as though the universe had stopped expanding, waiting for me to act, and now it had started moving and growing again. I licked a salty drop of perspiration from my upper lip and suddenly felt like a ravenous animal, the cutting tension of my panties against my tender flesh almost more than I could bear. I froze, unable to move, seized by an overpowering delight as I was overwhelmed by sensations my body could not accommodate. I was hungry, but I could consume no more at the moment. I was satiated, gratified by anticipation itself. I could take no more. I could only wait.

An eternity seemed to pass before I took another tentative move towards my objective. Galen's trousers were twisted slightly around his calf, and the sight of the pulled cloth aroused me. I imagined his tanned skin, hairy and firmly muscled beneath the expensive looking material. I wanted him to stretch his leg towards me, to caress me with it, to save me the agony of approaching him, but I knew it was my duty to keep moving. I edged along like a cat, lifting first my right hand with my right knee, and then my left hand with my left knee. Each move pressed the material of my panties against my pussy and my head spun from the delicious torture. I wanted to crawl forever, never reaching my goal but always having it in sight.

25

In the end I could not hold back. I lowered my left arm, bending it at the elbow, stretched my neck out and let the side of my face glance against his leg. Emboldened, I pressed my cheek more firmly against his calf and detected the warmth of his flesh against my own. I rubbed my face up and down his leg, feeling as though I could literally purr. I pressed my cheek against his trousers and felt the material crease beneath my warm skin. I nudged my shoulder against him, longing to fold myself around his leg. I wanted to curl around it so tightly he would never be able to shake me off. He did not speak or move or react in any way, and the way he deliberately ignored my actions mysteriously heightened my senses and drove me on.

I heard the muted roar of the crowd and even seemed to smell the tang of the bull's sweat, but they were distant impressions, messages from another world. My nerves were loaded down with the strangely delectable experience of my absolute humiliation. I was drowning, unable to breathe and gasping for air, overwhelmed by the waves of excitement crashing through me as a result of my body's subtle contact with my master's leg. I was sinking, drifting down to the ocean floor, the way he ignored me an anchor around my heart pulling me down into the depths of despair even as it elevated me to heights of desire I had never imagined possible.

Then I saw a hand reach down for me. I lifted my face and rubbed my cheek against it. I licked it, running my tongue along the smooth fingers. I licked the firm palm and buried my face in it. I pressed my eyes against the back of the hand one after another, closing them and imagining I was seeing the soul inhabiting the godlike form graciously extending his hand down to me from a more elevated dimension. The fingers stretched and I drew back, staring at them, waiting for their instructions. One finger pointed stiffly downwards. I bent my elbows and lowered my face to the floor. I felt again the delight brought on by my up-thrust buttocks and parted my knees slightly to accentuate the sense of exposure the angle gave me. I rested my cheek against the floor, my arms bent around my head, panting and waiting, hoping this moment of stillness would never end and I would never have to feel the loss of my growing excitement.

I hardly remember how long I stayed that way before the light-blue silk sashes were tied around my wrists and ankles. When I first felt them touch my skin, my eyes closed and I seemed to rise weightless into the air. I quivered as I felt them being pulled tight, and my heart beat faster and harder as I heard the swishing sound of a loose end being led out and laid flat on the floor. I was still crouching on my hands and knees, my right cheek pressed against the wooden boards. There was a tug on the ribbon around my left ankle and I opened my eyes, but I did not move my head. All I could see was a man's black shoe. I did not know whether it was Galen's or Mora's. I heard the roar of the crowd, but the sound only entered me through my left ear as in my right ear I felt a drumming through the boards as though the crowd was trying to break their way through to me.

I felt another sash being wound around my left elbow before being led across my back and tied off around my right elbow. My cheek still pressed firmly against the floor, I realised I could no longer move my upper arms at all. I

26

suffered a moment of panic, but it was immediately overtaken by a surge of the most extraordinary feeling of contentment. I would not have believed it possible to become even more sensually attuned to my surroundings, but I did. I felt the edges of my pussy pulsing against the tight material of my panties as a hand reached down and lifted the free end of the sash around my left wrist, and then another hand took hold of the right sash. They were lifted up from beneath the table and I felt the pull as they were wrapped around something. I felt a slight tension on the sashes at my ankles, and I knew they were being similarly secured. I bit my lip listening to the roar of the crowd, imagining Espartaco dancing before the bull as he confused it with his beauty and his finesse.

A sudden tug on the sashes around my wrists pulled my hands up off the floor, and as they stretched taut my head and chest were lifted into the air. The back of my shoulders touched the underside of the tabletop and I was transfixed beneath it with my head hanging down. Then the sashes at my ankles were pulled and my legs were also hoisted off the floor. I was suspended beneath the table, pressed firmly against it and completely unable to move anything but my head. Then suddenly the table scraped across the boarded floor of the box as it was pushed up, taking me with it. I cried out in fear, closing my eyes, and I heard Galen's voice.

'Syra, my pet, do not look down. Lift your head and keep your eyes open until I tell you otherwise.'

I lifted my head, and saw below me the arena with the blood-streaked bull and Espartaco in his dazzling suit and thousands of people clapping and stamping in a fevered tumult. As I hung there, exposed for all to see, bound and helpless, a seemingly endless orgasm surged through me, blinding me like another hot sun rising directly between my legs and exploding inside me.

Finally, my intense climax drained itself in the moisture seeping from my pussy and making my labia stick to my panties. I felt the drenched cotton being pulled aside. I don't know who it was touching me. It could have been anyone, Mora, Eve, Galen or even someone from the crowd. I did not care. The thin gusset was tugged away from my sex, which was spread wide by my position against the table, and a wave of hot air blew across my sensitised flesh like a desert wind. My clitoris, still throbbing with joy, sent pulsing waves of delight through my whole body as I stared out at the wild crowd and wished everyone in it was preparing to do whatever they wanted to me.

I clenched my teeth as something suddenly smacked my exposed pussy. I could do nothing to move away, I could not even squirm I was tied so securely. Another stinging blow fell directly between my thighs and I clenched my teeth. Another vicious slap stunned me and my throbbing labia burned with pain. I was being beaten with a leather belt. I could feel the unyielding smoothness of it and its hard tip lashing around the side of my right buttock, curling into my straining hip. A fourth blow fell across my helplessly exposed cunt and I bit my lip in order not to cry out, but with each successive lick of leather across my sex it became harder and harder not to scream in anguish. Yet I wanted to contain the pain, to hold it in and soak it up so it penetrated every part of my body,

27

working its way into my every blood cell. My cheeks were burning with tears by the time the belt finally stopped tormenting me. I heard it tossed aside and everything went quiet in my head, the roar of the crowd becoming confused with the sound of my own blood pounding through my temples and down into my pelvis as another blinding climax made my body convulse against the table.

CHAPTER 5

He was very angry with me for writing the word *cunt* again. He scratched it out with his red pen and then stared at me for a frighteningly long time. I could tell he was trying to decide what to do with me. He seemed puzzled, as though he could not find the answer he sought, as though simply spanking me was not enough, as though I needed something more than a mere beating.

In the beginning he always knew what to do with me, what punishment to give me, how to reprimand me, but now there are times when I can tell he is not at all sure any more what will work with me. Then suddenly he asked me if I wanted my wrists and ankles bound and a rope tied around my waist so I could be suspended from a hook in the ceiling. I nodded, and he shook his head. He asked me if I wanted to be tightly lashed to a post and whipped with a leather flail. I nodded again, and he shook his head again. He asked me if he should blindfold me then tie the ball gag he sometimes uses on me around my head and leave me like that until the next time he came to see me. Again I nodded, and as I did so, I felt the moisture of excitement seeping between the lips of my pussy. He asked me if there was anything he could think of that I would not want, and I slowly shook my head. I knew there was no way he could punish me that would bring me anything but intense delight. He asked me if I was beginning to feel pain again, and I nodded yet again, and as I thought of his spanking hand and the flailing whip and of how my body would strain against the bonds he promised me, how I would gulp for breath against the plugging gag as each smack, each lash, fell hard against my buttocks... I pressed my fingers against my throbbing clitoris and climaxed violently...

He has gone now. He seemed to get the answer he was searching for and left me without doing anything to me. There is a hollow sensation in my stomach, a gripe of terrible disappointment. But even though he did not beat me, I am consoled by the feelings the loss of punishment and its excitement have given me. It was not so long ago I thought I would never feel anything again.

I do not know how long I hung against the table in the president's box, I only know I remember it was lowered into a horizontal position again, and the deep feeling of sadness that accompanied being hidden from view. I would like to have struggled when they freed me, because I wanted to remain bound and helpless, but I knew I must only do what was wished of me. If I fought against them I would not feel so exquisitely degraded and the loss of my humiliation

28

would lessen my excitement.

At least when they sat me down on one of the chairs they kept my elbows tied tightly across my back. At least they did not release me completely. At least they allowed me to endure the tension in my arms a little longer and left the blue ribbons dangling from my wrists and ankles so I could be reminded of how I had been bound and exposed and beaten in front of thousands of people. My hands were resting up near my shoulders, but now I let them drop slowly and straightened my back so the sash holding my elbows slipped a little lower. My nipples were so hard against the thin material of my dress they ached for attention. Galen looked at them, and I shyly dropped my eyes.

'Syra, are you ashamed of your body?'

I shook my head without looking up.

'I *do* hope not. It would be such a shame. Syra, look up, do not be embarrassed.'

I raised my head.

'Look around you. What do you see?'

I turned my head and saw hundreds of faces staring at me from the terraces on either side of the presidential box. I felt the deep heat of a blush rising up my neck and covering my face, setting my cheeks and forehead aflame. It was as though their eyes were penetrating me like red-hot needles. I prickled all over, my heart pounded, and my nipples hurt even more as they pressed against my dress.

Eve moved into my line of sight. She leaned against the balustrade, her back to the arena, dropped her weight onto one hip and glared at me. She took off her sunglasses, licked one of her fingers and rubbed spit onto one of the lenses to clean it while I imagined it was her pussy and I was licking it. She pulled up the hem of her skirt to dry the lens while I stared at her thighs. She put the sunglasses back on, turned and looked down into the arena. 'Espartaco wins again,' she declared in a bored voice. 'What's new?'

Galen looked down at the scene as a wild roar issued from the crowd. 'A good victory, Mora. Look, the crowd is very pleased with the performance of the bull, and Espartaco can do nothing wrong for them. Look how he struts before them. See how he preens himself. Look how his fans cheer his expertise, his dazzling style, his panache and, most of all, his fearlessness. His courage is beyond their reach. It is what makes him seem like a god.' He turned his head and stared at me. 'Would you like to meet this god, Syra? Would you like to be in the presence of the god I have created?'

I pulled my elbows forward slightly to increase the delectable discomfort in my shoulder blades. 'Yes,' I replied quietly.

I felt the penetrating stares of the crowd again and looked to my left. Men were gawping at me, some were pointing, a few were clapping and several were laughing. I opened my mouth vacantly, submissively, as if I wanted to suck all their cocks at once.

'Good,' Galen said. 'Here, let me release you.'

I continued to stare back at the men as the sash came loose at my back. My shoulders dropped forward as the tension was released, and Galen took each of my wrists in his hands and placed them gently on my knees. The sashes still wound around them trailed over the sides of my thighs and touched the backs of my calves. I gripped the hem of my dress and held it tightly against the tops of my thighs. I felt as though I was preparing to face a cataclysm, a terrible force equivalent to an emotional hurricane.

Eve leaned out over the balustrade. She removed her sunglasses again and licked her finger to wet the other lens. She rubbed it, but when she put the glasses back on she was apparently dissatisfied with the result for she took them off again, turned, and held the inner side of the lens in front of my mouth. 'Wet it for me,' she ordered haughtily.

I flicked my tongue out and almost touched the glass before it was abruptly snatched away. 'Leave her alone!' Galen commanded angrily. 'She is not yours to play with.'

Eve scowled, and tossed the sunglasses down on the table.

I gripped the hem of my dress even more tightly, deafened by the roar of the crowd as Espartaco climbed up into the presidential box.

The entire bullring vibrated with the stamping of feet and the clapping of hands. Espartaco shone in the sunlight as if he had fallen out of a star. The sequins on his jacket flashed so brightly the rays emanating from them seemed to set fire to the red curtains draped around the box. Red, green and gold streaked from their dazzling points, beaming spots of light across my skin and daubing me with living colour as though I had tumbled into a vast kaleidoscope. This fiery god held his hat in the crook of his arm and bowed to Mora and Galen. He bent sharply at the waist, dropped his head low and scraped the edge of his hat against the floor. His tight trousers bulged against the straining pressure of his muscular thighs, and as he straightened up, they pressed so closely against his crotch that all the beautiful contours of his cock squeezed into the black material were revealed in tantalising detail. I could see the heavy, venous ribs running along the shaft and the wide glans at its tip, shaped like a delectable bell.

'Syra, my pet,' Galen said, 'meet the fearless Espartaco.'

The bullfighter stepped towards me and took one of my hands. My fingers still held the edge of my dress, so as he lifted my hand towards his mouth my dress rose as well. He smiled almost bashfully and looked away as my white panties were revealed. I let go of the hem, and as if nothing untoward had happened, he drew my hand to his mouth, pressed his full lips against it then gave it back to me gently and gracefully, as if my own hand was a gift from him.

'It is an honour to meet you, *senorita*,' he intoned in a deep voice with a heavy Spanish accent.

I felt myself trembling.

'Sit, please,' Mora urged, 'and have a drink with us. You have fought well, even though your first challenger was not a worthy opponent.'

Espartaco sat down beside me.

'No, indeed not, *presidente*. Espartaco does not have to kill the bulls that face

30

him, for some of them die from fear!'

'You are right, Espartaco,' Galen's voice was flatteringly smooth. 'What it must be like to be so fearless and so feared.' He sighed.

The bullfighter tossed his head back arrogantly and the gold clasp around his small pigtail flashed blindingly in the sun. His hands were resting on his knees and I could feel the heat of his skin against my leg. The tanned fingers were covered in thick black hairs and I wanted to touch them, to feel them lightly brushing my skin, so I edged my knee closer to his. 'I am indebted to you, Galen,' he declared. 'You have led me out of fear into courage. You have convinced me of my power and my invincibility. It is you who have found the fearlessness within me and released it.'

Galen nodded humbly. 'Perhaps,' he began, sipping his wine, 'you can describe how it feels to be beyond fear to my new pet, Syra. She wants to know how she can overcome her fears. She wants to lift herself above them and be guided into ecstasy only by the desires released from deep within her own being.'

'All I can say is that you have created me as I am, Galen,' Espartaco went on earnestly. 'When I take on the bull, I do not hear the crowd, I do not hear the panting of the beast before me, I do not smell the last victim's blood in the ring, I feel only the light inside me, the light of fearlessness you have helped me light.'

'Bravo!' Mora exclaimed. 'Bravo! *Maravilloso*! Marvellous!'

I edged my knee a little closer to his and felt warm air between my legs as they parted. I was nearly touching his hand now, and I saw him stretching his forefinger out, reaching for me as though he, too, desperately wanted to touch me. I looked down and watched my leg trembling. I did not know if I could move it, if I was still able to control my body. I felt a surge of anxiety in my belly and edged a little closer to him. The instant my knee touched his - and it was only the slightest glance - I felt a responsive pressure from the tip of his finger. He pressed the side of his thigh against mine, and I pressed back. I felt his nail digging into my flesh and leaned my leg against his as firmly as I could. The tip of his finger dug deeply into my skin, until I could not see his nail at all. I felt myself exhaling as though I would never be able to take another breath, and dropped my chin against my chest as I gasped involuntarily.

'Are you all right, Syra?' Galen asked me.

I nodded, coughing stupidly and blinking my eyes as if dazzled by the light caught in my lashes. I assumed he could see Espartaco's finger on my knee, and that this was why he had brought him up here. He was giving me another chance - a chance to make up for my idiocy on the beach. This was my opportunity. I could redeem myself here in the presidential box set high above the roaring crowd. I could prove to him I was of some value, that his efforts would not be wasted on me. But he would not instruct me. I would have to act only on the faintest clues he provided, on the slightest impressions I received from his gestures and expressions.

Being careful not to relieve any of the pressure of Espartaco's finger on my knee, I twisted my hips and moved the leg he was not touching further away from the other. I felt the gusset of my panties stretching against my pussy. I felt as though my clitoris was bulging out of its protective cover and pressing against my damp panties, exposing itself to the fullest sensation possible. I could feel my anticipation simmering in my clit as imagination drove my body to new levels of pleasure. I squeezed my buttocks together and twisted my hips again, pulling on the cotton covering my vulva with my clenched buttocks and drawing it hard against my warm and swollen flesh. It was not a pleasure derived from something or someone else, it was a determined, forceful action with only one focus - my own gratification.

'Look,' Espartaco said as he got up abruptly and went to stand at the edge of the box. 'They are parading some of the bulls that have won their right to freedom. They are fine specimens, but of course none of them have ever met me! There is not a bull alive who could win the right to live when facing Espartaco.'

Eve was still leaning on the balustrade, and now Galen and Mora went and stood on either side of her. Espartaco beckoned to me and I rose with difficulty. Since stepping into the presidential box I had been in the grip of some mysterious trance. I went and stood not beside him but in front of him. I placed my trembling hands on the balustrade and looked down at the parade of bulls. All of them were frightening, heavily muscled creatures. They were decked with coloured ribbons and sashes, and led on leather leashes attached to rings in their noses by pairs of boys dressed in dark suits. Some of the animals with deep scars on their bodies pulled viciously against the rings in their noses and some of the smaller boys found it hard to keep them in line. One of the boys fell over as he struggled with his charge, and only narrowly escaped being trampled by rolling frantically out from beneath the animal's hooves. I gasped as he scrambled to his feet, but felt calmed and quickly distracted from the scene below by the reassuring pressure of the matador's powerful body against mine. He smacked my right buttock, giving it a short, sharp slap as though I was a favoured calf. The blow stung, but it was too brief, so I pushed my bottom back against him to show I wanted more.

He moved tightly against me, until I could feel every sequin in his beautiful jacket and every muscle compressed into his shiny black trousers. The pressure increased and I felt the bulge against my buttocks hardening. I felt his buried erection pressing into me, expanding in response to my softly yielding flesh, becoming engorged with need. His right hand fell on my hip and I became aware of the shape of my bone beneath his warm hand. His fingers stretched and found the hollow at the front of my hips, and his expert touch caused a wave of anxious excitement deep between my buttocks. His fingers stretched down slightly, straining to reach the depression leading into the groove of flesh between the top of my thigh and the base of my stomach. My body throbbed with anticipation, and I tensed as his hand folded around my hip and his fingers stretched further. I turned slightly towards him, and his finger stroked the delicate flesh between my thigh and my pudenda, inflaming me. He stroked the edges of my pussy softly, tantalizing it and heating it up as if his fingers were

32

naked flames. I felt my labia blooming at the proximity of his touch, and as my sex lips swelled my eyes rolled up into my head as though I was going to faint. I wanted him to grab my cunt, all of it, to cradle its soft, pouting flesh and hold it in his hand until I came, but I knew he would not permit me such a simple, effortless release. He pressed his body harder against my back and squeezed me against the balustrade so tightly, I could not move as he kept stroking the delicate edges of my labia. But his fingers did not venture beyond this fleshy barrier. I panted with need and frustration. I felt his eager hard-on digging into my bottom cheeks and sensed its rhythmic throbbing as it continued enlarging and poking me through his tight pants. I tried to move back against it, to open my buttocks a little and accept it, but he would not let me. I opened my mouth, wanting to beg him to release me from this unbearable tension of desire, to give me his hand, his fingers, his throbbing, fleshy cock, anything that would penetrate me and allow me the relief of an orgasm, but no words came. I could not speak. I could scarcely breathe. I was drowning in a sea of fire and he was not going to rescue me. I could not find a way to make him open the petals of my labia. I could not find a way to encourage him to insert just the tip of his finger into my pussy. I could not make him find my aching clitoris and press down on it long enough for me to find relief from the consuming tension of my burning lust. I could do nothing. I was his victim, his slave, completely under his control. I pushed back against the bulge between his legs and felt his erection stiffen even more. With his hand so close to my sex I could feel its heat, and like a girl touched for the first time, the sensation was enough to make me start coming...

Suddenly the pressure of his body was no longer there. I felt alone and exposed, but not to him, to the world. A hand grabbed my arm and swung me round. I hoped to see the bullfighter staring down at me, preparing to be rough with me. Perhaps the tantalising gentleness of his hand had only been a prelude to his passionate strength. I longed to sacrifice myself to his power and thereby helplessly submit to my own ecstasy, but it was Galen who spun me angrily round to face him.

'You have made a nonsense of my hopes for you, Syra,' he accused me. 'You have allowed your pitiful desires to overcome you and have wasted them needlessly. Don't you understand that you have committed yourself to me? I cannot allow you to be involved with anyone else yet.'

My pussy was still throbbing, but instead of filling me with the need to release my passions the sensation made me feel hollow and degraded. I wanted to beg him for forgiveness. I wanted to tell him I thought he would be pleased with me if I let Espartaco play with me, for it would show my willingness to be bad and obey him. I felt ashamed as I realised how stupidly I had behaved. 'Galen, I am so...'

'Quiet!' he shouted angrily. Pulling me to him, he turned me sideways and slipped his left arm around my waist, pushing me forward over it. Then he lifted my dress and roughly yanked my panties down to my knees, making it clear the punishment for my misbehaviour would consist of more than words. He tilted

33

my bottom upwards, lifting my feet off the floor, and when he finished positioning me so anyone looking up into the presidential box could see my exposed buttocks, he brought his open palm down against them.

He subjected me to a succession of punishing smacks, beneath which my whole body tensed as I squirmed in the crook of his arm. The sharp sound of the spanking blended with the deep roar of the crowd, and with each stinging blow I felt myself more and more consumed by an unending orgasm. I imagined my reddened bottom, naked and displayed to the crowd, and the mere thought was enough to fuse one explosive rush of bliss into another. In the end I hung draped across his arm completely limp, dissipated by my own absolute pleasure and humiliation.

When he finished punishing me, Galen looked at Mora as he led me, staggering, out of the presidential box. To my disappointment the bullfighter had gone, apparently not interested in watching a girl being disciplined. 'Espartaco will not get any more approved bulls,' he announced. 'See to it. It is time for the great Espartaco to show us what he is really made of. It is time to see if my experiment has truly worked.'

The president nodded and Galen tugged on my arm as I stumbled behind him before regaining my balance. Then suddenly my eyes fell on someone I had seen before. The man in the Hawaiian shirt was leaning on an iron balustrade staring down into the noisy crowd below him. I followed his line of sight, and saw it ended at a young woman with long, sun-bleached blonde hair waving her programme and screaming at the top of her lungs.

She was standing on a low wall raising her slightly above everyone else, and she was trying desperately to get someone's attention. Every time she shouted, she flung her arm over her head and her thin dress pulled against her pert breasts, causing her hard nipples to strain against the taut material. As her desperation increased and she waved her arm more frantically, the hem of her dress hiked up around her thighs until I could see the cheeks of her bottom squeezing together as she lifted herself up on her toes, and for a tantalising moment I even glimpsed the bright whiteness of her panties. Then my arm was suddenly tugged hard as Galen pulled me into the dark exit tunnel.

It was cooler outside by the time I stepped through the tall doors of my master's house. That was the first time I saw the inner terrace - a hexagonal white-tiled area full of large potted plants surrounding the base of a spiralling chromium staircase winding up to the second floor. It was as if the ancient town of irregular whitewashed houses was only a façade designed to hide an ultra modern home transplanted there from the future.

'Stay here,' he ordered as he let go of me and ran lithely up the steel staircase.

I stood there waiting for him obediently. I was glad Eve had remained back at the stadium and I did not have to compete with her for his attention. It was the first time I had felt cool since I arrived in Spain, and I shivered. I ran my hands down over my hips and then up again. My panties were lodged in my bottom crack, and after hesitating a moment, I slipped a finger between the gusset and

34

my skin and pulled them to one side, exposing my pussy. I seated myself on a cool marble bench surrounded by large potted ferns, and my dress rose up at the back as I sat down, enabling me to relish the sensation of cold stone against my warm flesh.

CHAPTER 6

He did not like what I had written. *No*, he wrote across the word *cunt*, and in the margins added, *If you ever use this word again you will be punished for disobedience.* I watched him writing angrily and felt genuinely frightened. When I realised what I was feeling I experienced another surge of fear, and that brought on another one. It was as though I was tumbling down an endless hill, out of control, helplessly thrilled by my own anxiety. I wanted to shout to him, 'Go on then, punish me. Do whatever you want to me. Beat me. Tie me up. Whip me. Gag me. Blindfold me. Hang me up from ropes. Do anything you want to me. Do it! I want it. Don't you understand? I want it! I can feel fear again. My senses have returned!' But I said nothing, and when he left, I carried on dutifully with my work.

Minutes later I was startled by his return. I put my pencil down and looked up nervously as he stood on the threshold with several thin ropes hanging dangling from his hands. He told me to crawl over to him and kneel before the step leading up to the door. I did as I was told, shuffling across the cold floor, looking all the time at the ropes. He told me to turn my head sideways and lay my cheek on the step. The bricks were cold against my skin and I could taste mortar dust in the corner of my mouth. He told me to put my arms behind my back, and as soon as I did he began binding them together with one of the ropes, so tightly I could feel my hands throbbing with blood. He straddled me, facing my upturned bottom, bent down and tied the remaining ropes around my knees and ankles.

He crouched above me and I could feel the heat of his genitals between my shoulder blades, then he rubbed his hand across my taut buttocks. His palm felt smooth and hot as he massaged my skin, testing its resilience, searching out my curves so when he brought his hand down it would land in just the right place and cover as much flesh as possible. He slipped a finger into my crack and pressed the tip against the opening of my anus. He circled the hard muscle, and then pushed his digit inside me. I gasped softly as it penetrated, but no sooner had he slipped his finger past my clenched ring than he pulled it out again. He took his hand away completely, and there was a moment's silence before the first blow fell, hard and punishing, across my left buttock. Next he spanked my right buttock with even more force, and I clenched my cheeks in readiness for the next searing impact. When his hand came down again it was harder still, and he continued spanking me that way, alternating between my left and right cheeks until I thought I would pass out from the mingled pain and ecstasy. Then

35

he untied me and left me alone again.

I did not have to wait long for Galen to come back down the stairs. He was excited and his anger had vanished. I was pleased his mood had changed, but it was also a warning to me that his temperament was extremely volatile and I should never assume anything in the future.

'Everything is ready, Syra my pet. You do not have to wait any longer.' Smiling, he took my hand and invited me to stand. I did so, and he led me to the base of the spiral staircase. The hem of my dress had barely dropped enough to cover my bottom, and my panties were still squeezed tightly between my buttocks and pulled aside so my pussy was exposed to the delicious air-conditioning.

He indicated the stairs and I began climbing the shiny, twisting steps as he followed behind me. As I went higher, my perspective of the inner terrace below me altered. It broadened out so I could see the wide spaces between the plants and objects placed between them - small tables holding statues or orchids in small glass vases. I did not look behind me at him, but he was so close I could feel the heat of his body. My panties pulled against the left edge of my pussy, and every time I lifted my leg to the next step it tightened deliciously.

I reached the second floor and stopped, my heart racing. I wanted him to move closer to me now. I wanted him to lift my dress and stare at my sex while I stood motionless on the landing. I wanted to lift my leg onto the chrome banister and expose myself completely to his scrutiny. I wanted to hear him describe me, the softness of my flesh, its pinkness, the shape of my outer labia, how my lips folded so neatly into my pussy with only the slight crease of skin covering my clitoris breaking the perfectly defined line. I wanted him to tell me to spread my legs even wider, as wide as I could. I wanted him to reach up and pull apart the lips of my labia and expose the darker pink of the inner flesh, holding them open so I could feel their warm wetness against the cool dry air. I wanted him to put his face between my straining legs and stare as closely as he desired at my aching, moistening sex. I wanted him to reach out with his tongue and flick its tip against my clitoris. I wanted him to run the probing point around its sensitive edges and then, as it became inflamed, to abandon it, leaving it throbbing with frustration as he used his whole tongue to lap my vulva like a thirsty, ravenous beast...

'Go on, Syra,' he urged. 'I want you to see the city.'

I moved forward, my eyes filled with light. Half of the room was covered with a high, vaulted ceiling while the rest stretched out over a large open balcony jutting out like a vast diving board across the street below. The floor of both the room and the balcony was constructed from a highly polished cherry-red timber. Two fans spun lazily on floor stands and a palm tree in a stainless steel pot sat near the edge of the balcony. In the centre of the room was a raised hexagonal platform made from the same red timber as the floor. In the top of the platform there was a tightly closed split and a large, chromium-plated padlock hanging across a shiny hasp and staple at its centre. A good-sized chromium-plated cupboard with two upper doors, two lower ones and two drawers in between,

36

stood alongside the raised platform. There were two doors in the far wall of the room, one red and one green.

'May I?' I asked, looking towards the balcony.

'Of course, of course, go ahead, but be careful, there is no rail.'

I walked out onto the balcony and the full force of the setting sun shone upon me. I felt my shoulders burning in its red heat and pulled my hair back tightly with both hands to let my features bask in its radiance. The star's intensity burned my cheeks and caused flashing lights to dance across my closed eyelids. I looked away, slightly dizzy, and moved closer to the edge of the balcony. I looked out over the city, its complex of narrow streets a maze of white-walled and red-roofed houses. In the distance I could make out a large square with imposing buildings surrounding it, and everywhere I looked I could see the spires of churches poking up like spears on a blood-soaked battlefield. A much smaller square lay below the balcony, and people sat in the shady corners of cafes and the dry green trees surrounding them. I felt giddy as I stepped closer to the edge, and for a moment imagined I must reach out and support myself on the rail I knew was not there. A surge of fear paralysed me as I realised how easily my mind confused reality with imagination, and I stepped back quickly.

Galen laughed quietly. 'I know what you were doing sitting on the marble bench,' he told me. 'I watched your expression.'

I felt a flush of shame warm my cheeks.

'Yes, you should realise by now, Syra, that I know everything you feel. It is already almost impossible for you to keep a secret from me. I watched it all. I saw you lift the hem of your dress so your bottom would be exposed to the chill of the stone. I watched you pull aside your panties so your pussy would be able to feel the marvellous, fresh sensation of coolness. I watched you wriggle with pleasure. I saw the look on your face as you pressed your bottom against that smooth, hard surface. Oh yes, I saw the look of commitment, of single-mindedness, of absorption in the sensation. Then I saw that you deliberately did not pull down your dress when you started up the stairs. But Syra, I did not look as you walked in front of me up the stairs. Did you think I did? I hope you are not disappointed. I hope I have not reduced your pleasure. Oh my, I can see I have let you down. But you are so simplistic. There is so much to be done with you.'

I felt annoyed. I felt he was trying to make me look stupid. 'I didn't imagine for one second that you were looking,' I lied defensively, and felt even more stupid.

'Oh Syra,' he sighed, 'come and sit here.' He indicated the raised platform in the centre of the room. 'Remember, being truly bad is what you have come to learn how to do. I do not expect you to be bad yet. I only expect you to be a good student. Are you going to be a good student, Syra?'

I could do nothing but nod.

'Good.' He studied me soberly. 'Good,' he repeated, seeming convinced by my expression.

I felt strangely hesitant to approach the raised platform. It looked ominous, as though beneath what looked like a hatch there lay something terrible, something shocking.

'Afraid?' he asked me sharply. 'Surely not, Syra.'

'No, I - I'm not afraid,' I stammered.

'Well, we shall see. Perhaps being so close to Espartaco has made you brave? Perhaps some of his fearlessness has rubbed off on you?'

I suspected he was mocking me, but nevertheless I found myself speechless in the face of his dark, sinister charm.

'Although I do hope not, for his sake,' he added wryly. 'He will need all his courage from now on.'

'What do you mean?'

'I mean that the next time Espartaco goes into the ring, he will need to draw on even the tiniest bit of courage you might have stolen from him. I think the next bull he faces will be more of an opponent than he has been used to so far. But Syra, come and sit.' He patted the platform, indicating the place he wished me to sit even as he lowered himself onto it.

I shivered slightly, and then went and sat beside him. 'What is this?' I asked, stretching towards the shiny padlock.

He reached out quickly and slapped the back of my hand. The blow hurt, and I winced and pouted as I snatched my hand back.

'You must not touch that, Syra my pet.'

'Why not?' I demanded petulantly, rubbing my reddened skin.

'Because you are my student and it is enough that I have told you not to touch it.'

'But I've been trained to ask questions. It's my *job*,' I retorted. 'I'm a student of psychology.' My tone was assertive, as though reminding myself of what I was, or had been, would somehow make things normal again. It did not.

'Then being my student should be easy for you,' he replied mildly. 'Once I had many students. I worked at a famous university, but they did not appreciate my talents. Now I do my research here. *This* is my laboratory.' He looked around the room, smiling. 'And you are my special student, Syra. Now bend over. My student needs her bottom spanked for insolence.'

I felt my eyes opening wide in disbelief, but I merely enquired submissively, 'Where?'

'Over my knee, of course, like a naughty student.' He rose and seated himself in a chrome-framed chair. 'Here.'

I walked over to him slowly, my eyes lowered. I felt guilty and naughty as he patted his knees and I bent over them without hesitating. I stretched my hands to the floor and allowed my hips to rest fully on his lap. My panties drew up tightly into my pussy and I wondered whether he would pull them down or simply peel them to one side. He pulled them down. I shivered with excitement as I felt the flimsy white material dragging against my skin, and then twisting like a soft rope halfway down my thighs. He paused to look closely at my upturned buttocks as though analysing them, judging their muscular tone and their smoothness to determine how hard they should be spanked. Perhaps he was

38

wondering how quickly they would redden beneath his admonishing hand. Because of the angle I was lying at, I knew he could see my anus and the outer edges of my pussy, and I squirmed slightly in an effort to show him more.

He placed his hand firmly against the small of my back to hold me still. 'Your bottom is very smooth,' he observed. 'It is pale, though, and I will not stop until it is bright red.'

I allowed my buttocks to relax, saving the joy of tensing them for the moment when I felt his hand coming down against them. He carried on caressing and priming them for a while, and then he lifted his hand. I waited, breathing fast and biting my lip in anticipation. I wondered how hard he would spank me and whether there would be a prescribed number of blows. Wondering only intensified my excitement and I lifted my buttocks slightly, holding my breath.

He did not speak nor count nor explain to me again why I was being punished. He simply swept his hand down over and over again with relentless regularity. Each blow made me jolt, but the stinging pain of his flesh impacting with mine was the most powerfully wonderful sensation. I did not count how many times he spanked me. All I know is that my discipline for being insolent went on for a very long time, more than long enough for me to climax violently, shuddering and writhing on his lap.

He stopped punishing me and let me roll off his knees. I fell onto my side at his feet, and groaned when my burning bottom touched the floor as I rolled over onto my back. I looked up at him, not knowing whether he had finished with me, not knowing whether I should show how him much I was hurting and how much more I wanted him to hurt me.

'Now, Syra my pet,' he said casually, 'you must freshen up, take a bath and shave your pubic hair. That is why I did not look between your legs when you walked in front of me up the stairs. How could I?'

'Where is the bathroom?' I asked at once.

He pointed to the green door. 'You will find everything you need in there.'

I got up, making an effort not to wince and reach behind me to cradle my burning cheeks, and walked over to the green door. The smooth round metal handle was cool in my hand, and I stood there for what seemed like ages frozen at the point of action but unable to act. It was as though holding the handle but not turning it would somehow save me from my fate. As long as I stood there motionless nothing would happen. I would retain control over my actions... I turned the handle and walked through the door.

There were no windows in the room I entered, and all the walls and the entire floor were covered with brilliant white tiles. Bright lights set in the ceiling lit up every object with icy intensity; every edge was picked out clearly and every shadow perfectly defined. A chrome showerhead was fixed to a shiny silver pipe emerging from the ceiling, and a circular steel ring hung with a white curtain was set below it. Beside it, on a metal stand, was a bar of soap and a razor.

I pulled off my dress, letting it fall to the floor in a crumpled heap, and tugged the thin gusset of my panties back across the flesh of my pussy before sliding them down my hips. My labial lips were still sensitive to the caress of the sticky

39

material as it came away, and I ran one finger slowly against my slit. I felt my clitoris blooming between the fleshy mounds surrounding it, and when I pressed my fingertip against it, I felt its subtle heat. Then behind me I heard the green door opening.

'Do I have to watch you all the time just to be sure you do what you are told?' Galen demanded.

'No,' I said quickly, pulling my panties all the way down and stepping out of them. I stepped into the shower without turning around, but when I glanced over my shoulder, I saw he had left and closed the door behind him. I reached up and turned a heavy knob. The water spurted from the showerhead and I jumped back as the freezing cascade hit my breasts. I shivered and stepped back even farther as my nipples immediately hardened and goose bumps covered my flesh. I pulled my shoulders together to try and suppress another shiver, then took a deep breath and stepped beneath the frigid flow. I tensed my whole body, tightening my chest and forcing my arms down my sides as I let the cold water soak me with its chilling torrent. It ran between my breasts and over my stomach, circling my navel and rushing in seemingly eager waves towards my vulva. I watched it threading through my blonde pubic hairs, teasing them out and dripping off their ends. I stood with my legs open and let the ice-cold stream curve like an eager river against the insides of my thighs. I lifted my face into the flow, and as I stood pulling back my hair with my hands, my body began feeling warmer. The icy water no longer felt like an enemy; I was attuned to it and welcomed it. I took the bar of soap from the stand and rubbed it against my pubic hair, producing a fragrant white froth that ran down the fronts and the insides of my thighs into my cunt. I rubbed the soap harder against me and stepped back out of the stream. Then I placed the soap back on the stand, picked up the razor and carefully applied the blade to my mound.

I paused a moment, for there was something about the act of shaving my pubic hair that seemed terribly final, as though I would never be the same again afterwards. I knew my hair would grow back, but it was not as simple as that. I felt that if I shaved my pussy I would lose a mysterious sort of innocence and virginity. I sliced off the first few hairs, and straight away experienced an electrifying excitement. I dragged the blade further, feeling the sharp edge against my skin, and was aroused by the risk involved in having a sharp surface grazing my delicate flesh. I sliced through my hair and saw my fresh, naked skin exposed for the first time over my pussy. It was almost more than I could bear; how clean and pure it looked.

I wished Galen had stayed to watch and glanced back at the door just in case he decided to return, but he did not.

When I had shaved off all the pubic hair I could see, I sat beneath the shower, opened my legs wide and shaved any hairs that remained by feel. When finished, I felt absolutely naked and utterly exposed. I was instantly turned on. I placed my hand flat against my pussy and stood up. I ran my finger against the smooth crack and it felt like a new cunt - like someone else's cunt. I felt a rush of excitement at the thought and let my finger part the unnaturally smooth flesh

40

and poke inside the warm, welcoming entrance.

I heard the door handle turn, and glancing over my shoulder caught Galen's eye as he looked around the edge. He looked angry and immediately I felt ashamed of how long I had lingered in the shower. 'Have I been too long?' I asked, quickly shutting off the water.

'Come here,' he said coldly.

'I'm sorry, I know I should have been quicker.' I looked around me for a towel and something to wear, but there was nothing.

'Come here!' he commanded impatiently.

I walked carefully across the cold tiles with my eyes lowered. 'I have shaved as you asked me to,' I told him meekly.

'I did not *ask* you to,' he corrected me fiercely, 'I *told* you to.' He opened the door and I walked into the main room without him having to tell me to. I stopped and waited for him, water dripping down my body and running onto the shiny red floorboards. By the time he closed the green door a puddle of water surrounded me, making me feel as though I had wet myself with fear waiting to see what he was planning next.

He walked past me and sat on the raised platform in the centre of the room. 'I thought I would ask Eve to join us,' he informed me, 'but I have decided not to.' His anger was gone again, but the menacing tone had returned. 'Go and stand on the balcony,' he instructed. 'It is a pleasant evening. The air is filled with fragrances. It will dry you as though you had been rubbed down by scented towels.'

I walked obediently towards the balcony, and as I approached it I did indeed feel my skin drying. The evening had cooled slightly but it was still balmy and warm and the air was soft with the approach of night. I stopped and looked back at him. 'Where shall I stand?' I asked submissively.

'Walk to the edge, Syra my pet, right to the edge.' He must have seen the fear on my face, but he gave no indication of it, simply waited for me to obey him.

My mouth went dry and my stomach clenched anxiously. I stepped forward, but suddenly my legs felt hollow and so weak I could not move any further. 'I'm afraid,' I admitted pitifully. 'I can't...'

'What frightens you the most, Syra? Is it the exposed edge of the balcony? Is it the fear of falling? Is it the fear of leaning on a rail that is not there? Or is it the fear of being seen from below, the fear of exposing your naked body to strangers, the fear of letting the world see your shaved pussy? Which is it, Syra?'

'I don't know,' I confessed, turning back to face the room.

'Why are you here, my pet? I thought you wanted to face your fears, to conquer them, to find out what it is to be truly bad, to look into yourself and discover what lies within you, to see if your evil intents are your passions or whether they are all just fantasies. Isn't that why you have come with me, Syra?'

I stopped and bit my lip. I was pathetic. My intentions kept crumpling at every challenge. I felt weak and miserable and wretched. 'How near the edge?' I asked purposefully.

'As close as you can get without falling, my pet.'

41

As I walked across the broad balcony I felt the increasing exposure, not only to the dangerous edge but also to the people slowly filling the square below. I heard their voices before I saw them greeting each other, ordering drinks and laughing. The sound filled my head and I imagined them waiting for me to appear like a newly married princess being presented by her lord to his subjects. As I neared the edge I felt the drop coming closer and my awareness of it frightened me, daunted me, but most of all what filled my mind was the thought of the penetrating stares waiting for my naked body to show itself.

'Stop there,' Galen commanded.

I stopped, and shivered with the ecstasy of being completely under his control as I dared to curl my toes over the edge of the balcony. The square was crowded with people, but my eyes immediately fell on the corner of a bar terrace next to a dark alley where a young, dark-haired woman with full red lips was sitting.

She leaned forward eagerly as she conversed with two young men who made her laugh with their responses. The soft, temperate air wafted up towards me, scented with the fragrances of evening. Each of the young men was under the girl's spell; their emotions controlled by her every movement. I watched her becoming increasingly self-assured as she hung on to both their arms for minutes at a time. She rested her forehead against theirs for a moment, bunting them like a fawn, and stroked their cheeks, pouting as she did so. She rested her hands on their laps and kissed each of them in turn, first on the cheek and then on the lips. And as I watched I could sense their increased knowledge of each other, their growing intimacy, until I felt myself becoming part of it. I sensed the heat of their bodies, felt the warmth of passion on their skin. I seemed to taste their lips as they pressed together and to feel their tongues as they probed the insides of each other's welcoming mouths. I watched as the girl, finally submitting to both men, was led from the terrace and around the corner into the dark alley. I saw one young man lift up her skirt and realised that, like me, she was not wearing panties and her pussy was shaved. I watched the young man kneel before her and lick her naked cunt while the other youth held her shoulders and kissed her, tonguing her deeply as she writhed in increasingly uncontrollable passion. I saw her being held against the wall by one of her suitors, her legs spread apart, as the other one opened the front of his trousers and promptly drove his hard cock up into her willing cunt. I watched her being steadied by one man as the other lifted her up in his arms and climaxed deep inside her. I saw her anxious face as he slipped out of her, and then the paradoxical keenness with which she accepted the second erection into her body, driving down over it until it, too, filled her with a pulsing stream of hot semen. I watched as she sank to her knees and sucked them both down, first one at a time for a while and then alternating between them. Then she blew them both at once, squeezing both cocks into her mouth and making them stiffen again. One of the men came over her face and the other sprayed his cum deep into her gaping, wanton mouth.

All the time I watched this scene I stood perfectly still, my toes clinging to the edge of the balcony. My orgasm began when the first man opened his trousers

42

and it continued until the young woman smoothed down her dress and went back to sit on the terrace with her two lovers. Still I did not move, exhibiting myself like a statue to one of the young men as he glanced up inadvertently and saw me. As he stared I imagined myself as the young woman he had just fucked, and when I pictured myself being pressed against the wall by him as he drove his rigid cock into me, I felt another climax cresting inside me.

He drew a red line through what I had written about being in the shower, and scrawled in capital letters across it, *IS THIS MORE FANTASY?* He passed the pages back to me and sat waiting. I shook my head and he did not say anything as he stared at me. I clenched my teeth and shook my head again firmly, but he still did not respond. I felt foolish and stared down at my knees. Finally he told me to lie on the floor on my back, and I did. The stone was cold and made me shiver. He told me to be still, to put my hands by my sides and stay there without moving until he returned.

I lay there for what felt like ages doing exactly as he had said, hardly allowing myself to breathe in case he came back suddenly and said I was not still enough. When he did finally return, he was carrying a steel-legged chair in one hand and a silver razor in the other. He placed the chair above my feet, sat on it and told me to open my legs until my ankles pressed against the thin legs of the chair.

'In the same way that you described yourself sitting in the shower,' he said.

He passed me the razor and told me first to shave my pubic hair and then to touch myself. He would judge whether what I had written was a fantasy according to how much pleasure I expressed.

My pubic hair had barely grown back from the last time he told me to shave. I pressed my ankles as hard as I could against the steel legs of the chair and began passing the blade over my mound. I was not afraid. I knew what I had written was true, and I knew, as I felt the dull pain of the steel legs against my ankles and the bite of the razor against my hairs, that it would not be long before he was convinced I had found the experience incredibly sensual.

He sat with his forearms resting on his knees, leaning slightly forward in the chair and staring down between my legs. He watched my fingers as I drew them up between my shaved crack, opening the outer lips of my sex and exposing the glistening pink inner flesh. I saw him lick his lips like a hungry wolf as I fondled my freshly shaved labial lips.

'You wrote that word again more than once,' he accused me abruptly. '*Cunt.*' Then he got up and left and I made myself come before carrying on with my work.

I do not quite remember how I got from the balcony into the small bed I found myself in the following morning. When I woke up I did not know where I was, then all of a sudden, like an explosion in my brain, it came back to me and I pressed my face deep into the pillow. All I could hear was my heart beating and the low snuffling sound of my breathing against the soft pillow; the rest of the world was silent. I felt cut off from everything, as if there was only me, and all the things I could see, touch, hear and smell were merely in my head, an incredibly vivid sensual dream. It was as if my mind had become detached from reality. I felt panicky, and sat up hoping sudden physical movement would put things right. My head ached as if I had drunk too much alcohol. I wiped my nose with the back of my hand, sniffing. I could not remember having a single drink. I got out of bed, ran to the door and grabbed the handle. It turned easily and the door opened. I had feared it would be locked. I walked out naked into the lower terrace of Galen's house, and looking up instinctively, I saw him leaning over the balustrade at the top of the spiral staircase.

'Syra, my pet, you're awake. Good. Come up for something to eat.'

I knew I was naked and for a second did not know what to do - go back and find something to wear or ignore my embarrassment. Being perfectly honest with myself, I acknowledged the latter scenario was truly my only option, and I began walking up the stairs. He took my hand for the last two steps, and I nodded my thanks to him for the gracious gesture. Everything seemed so normal and matter-of-fact this morning that I dared to smile at him as he let go of my hand. 'What shall I eat for breakfast?' I asked.

'Very little,' he replied, returning my smile as if my question amused him. 'Perhaps some orange juice, which is very fresh, and a small bread roll with olives. You can dip the bread into some warm olive oil. You will enjoy it.'

I sat down on one of the chrome chairs. It was cold against my naked bottom, and I liked that. I picked up the small bread roll laid out on a white napkin and dipped it into a bowl of olive oil sitting in the centre of the table. The silky, honey-coloured oil dripped from the bread as I lifted it away, soaking it through and making it even more soft and succulent. I held it above my mouth, allowing several drops of oil to fall onto my tongue before slipping it between my lips. I sucked on it, and the saturated dough dissolved on my tongue. It was warm and chewy and the oil, although not bitter, possessed an astringency that made me wince slightly. I dipped the rest of the bread in the bowl again and felt a warm shiny glow coating my lips. A trickle of oil ran down my chin and I picked up the napkin to rub it away, but I looked at Galen, knowing I should defer to his opinion before I did anything, and he shook his head. So I placed the napkin back on the table and dipped the bread in the glistening pool between us. A glint of reflected sunlight caught the sharply cut facets of the crystal bowl and shone through the golden oil. I felt I wanted to bathe my naked body in it, to cover myself with it and drink it, to let it soak between my legs until I dissolved in a deep, warm orgasm. I took another bite of sopping bread and felt a rush of excitement deep within my pelvis.

'Where's Eve?' I asked casually.

'She is here,' Galen replied as the pet walked up behind him and rested her hands on his shoulders.

She stared past me over the balcony into the pastel-blue sky. She seemed lost in thought, detached and preoccupied with something more important than me. She blinked swiftly a few times as though trying to rouse herself, and then, refreshed by her effort, finally looked at me. Suddenly I felt self-conscious of

44

the oil running down my chin. I bent my head to hide it, and a bead of oil dripped between my breasts. She smiled a thin smile, and walking past me draped her long fingers against the oil on my chest, touching it fleetingly as an insect might land on the surface of a pond. I wanted her hand to move down to caress my stomach and cradle my shaved cunt, but she moved past me and walked out onto the balcony. I ate the last bit of oil-soaked bread and studied her as though she was an icon set against the sky to warn pilgrims of the dangers of the journey ahead.

She wore a loose-fitting, long red dress with a slit up the front ending high between her slender thighs. The neck was cut low in a deep V and the upper halves of the firm mounds of her breasts were exposed. The material of her dress was thin, and as she stood against the light I saw that apart from a tight thong she wore nothing beneath it. The long fingernails she clearly obsessed over were painted red and she wore a gold ring on her right forefinger. Her toenails were painted the same vivid bloody colour and she wore sandals that were merely flat soles tied to her feet with crossed red laces. Her bearing was one of peaceful stillness, of pure self-containment and absorption. I felt uncomfortably aware of my nakedness looking at her, and wanted to hide myself.

'We must get you ready to go out,' Galen announced, rising. 'It will be dark soon.'

I frowned in confusion. 'But it's only morning...'

'Syra, my pet, you have been asleep all day.'

I looked towards Eve and she sneered back at me over her shoulder as though I was beneath contempt. I looked out over the balcony and saw the deep red of the setting sun approaching the misty blue line of the horizon. I felt ridiculous and my cheeks flushed with the burning red of humiliation.

Galen led me back down the spiral staircase into the bedroom where I slept for so long, and Eve followed. He opened a wardrobe built into the wall and ran his hand across a range of dresses on hangers. I rushed forward; keen to see the clothes and even more keen to cover myself up.

'Not so fast,' he scolded mildly. 'We must be careful about what you wear. We are to meet two of my friends this evening. Eve will dress you. Do exactly as she says.'

The pet chose everything for me and laid it out on the unmade bed. Then she led me to the shower and watched while I cleaned myself. She brought some white nail varnish and told me to paint my toenails. I sat on the floor, pulling my feet up one by one onto the top of my thighs, and did as she said. Then she led me back into the bedroom and told me to get dressed in the clothes she had selected for me.

As I put them on I felt more embarrassed than I had before, as if the act of concealing it heightened my nakedness. Apparently she had decided I would not wear a bra or panties. I pulled on the white leggings, which were as thin and sheer as tights. The smooth elastic material drew up tightly around my buttocks and the seam at the crotch pulled into the fleshy crack between my legs. I lifted

45

my feet one at a time onto the edge of the bed and slipped on the white strap sandals with built up heels. They fitted perfectly and the smooth leather soles felt cool against the bottoms of my feet. I paraded around the room wearing only the leggings and sandals and Eve nodded her approval. I pulled on a loose red blouse that buttoned down the front and then painted my fingernails white. There was an awkward few minutes of silence while we waited for the polish to dry. The pet perched on the edge of the mattress studying her own immaculate fingernails while I stood balancing on my new high-heels, getting the feel for them. Finally, I judged it safe to pull on a pair of elbow-length white satin gloves.

There were no mirrors in the room, but as we crossed the downstairs hall I glimpsed myself in the shiny surface of a large chrome cupboard. I tilted back my head slightly as I saw my reflection, and sensed the pet sneering at me.

'Eve is not coming,' Galen informed me as he took my arm and turned his back on her indifferently. 'Let us go. We can walk from here. You will enjoy the lively nightlife, I'm sure.'

He led me through the bustling narrow streets, and although there was still some light in the sky it paled in comparison to the warm illumination flowing like liquid gold from every cafe, bar and restaurant we passed. Every so often someone acknowledged Galen with a nod or an uplifted hand and I felt like a favoured lover, my clothes radiant in the pools of light we walked between as if sailing from island to island in a dark sea. And the further we went, the more I wanted him to test my innate wickedness.

Every time we passed the corner of an unlit alley, I thought, I hoped and I dreaded he would ask me to enter it and wait in the seedy darkness. I imagined how I would stand in the alley, my heart pounding, until a group of men sent by my master arrived and threw me roughly to the ground. He would watch from the entrance of the alley as the men held me down and thrust their hard cocks into my pussy one after the other, violently banging me and pulling out only when they were ready to spray their hot semen all over my face. Then they would all fuck me again, this time coming in my mouth. When they finally got bored with me, they would pull me to my feet and make me bend over so they could beat me. I imagined how hard they would beat me and how painful the lash of the leather belt would be, or the cruel stinging cut of a cane. In the end they would shove me down onto the ground again and leave me, covered in their sticky semen, my white leggings ripped to shreds and my red blouse crumpled around me like dried blood. Galen would come to me finally and throw me a handkerchief to wipe my face, and I would feel degraded and ashamed as he called me a whore and a slut. When he had finished humiliating me with his words, I would crawl over to him on my hands and knees and beg him to bring me more men so it could happen all over again. He would call me an insatiable slut, but he would instruct me to wait and soon return with more men. I imagined it would be sunrise before he decided I had been sufficiently used and humiliated, and as it began to grow light he would drag me into the main square, force me onto all fours, and publicly beat me across the buttocks until I passed

46

out from exhaustion and ecstasy...

We passed through a dark entrance and entered a smoke-filled club with a low ceiling. A slim young woman dressed in light-blue shorts and a sleeveless white vest showing off her deep cleavage escorted us between a crush of tables.

'Now, Syra my pet, I do not want you to say anything. No matter what happens, you must not speak again until I tell you to do so.'

The young woman in shorts showed us to a table where two men were already sitting. One of them was attractive, his dark tan a stunning contrast to his silver hair. The other man was dark, square-jawed and swarthy, and was wearing a red and white Hawaiian shirt. I could scarcely believe it, but he was most definitely the man who watched me masturbating from the balcony and the man I saw at the bullring watching the blonde girl with the short dress. I hung my head, dreading he might say something about having seen me before. Both men were clearly Spaniards, but they greeted Galen in English. They shook hands with him, but ignored me. Obviously they had no intention of acknowledging me unless Galen introduced me, and I was relieved to think that perhaps the man in the Hawaiian shirt did not recognise me.

'This, my friends,' Galen said at last, 'is Syra. You may not have realised she was here, she has been so silent.'

Both men laughed, and the one in the Hawaiian shirt glared at me knowingly.

'Let me introduce you,' my new master went on. 'It seems a pity to exclude her from our conversation.'

The man with the light hair was introduced first. Gonzalo took my gloved hand in his and kissed it gallantly, and I was excited by my own silent and sophisticated nod of acknowledgement. But when the man from the balcony lifted my hand to his lips, he squeezed my fingers painfully and I knew he recognised me.

'You have embarrassed her, Juan Carlos,' Gonzalo accused his companion, observing my deep blush.

Juan Carlos said nothing, but merely smiled and kissed my hand again before releasing it.

They both seemed increasingly amused by the fact that I did not speak. As I nodded to each of them silently, the feeling of detachment I derived from my silence continued to excite me. I nodded like a doll, like a puppet on a string, and then sat listening to their conversation with wide, curious eyes.

'No, my friends,' Galen was saying, 'Espartaco will no longer receive the benefit of approved bulls.'

'Why is this, Galen?' Gonzalo asked. 'Surely you have not tired of Espartaco's victories? Have we not all profited from his courage and daring?'

'Yes, my dear Gonzalo, we have all profited well from his victories, but his courage and daring have not been exposed to the sort of challenges he thinks they have. I warned you at the beginning there would be a point at which I would have to let my experiment face his fear alone. Now, my friends, is the time.'

'As long as there is someone else who can benefit from bulls drugged into submission, then I suppose it does not matter,' Gonzalo said uncertainly. 'Espartaco can face his enemy, real or approved, it is irrelevant to us as long as our profits are not reduced.'

'One bet against Espartaco should set us all right,' Galen declared wryly, and all three men lifted their glasses in an amused endorsement of the plan.

'And Mora is in agreement?' Juan Carlos queried soberly.

'Yes, of course, of course,' Galen assured him.

I listened attentively as they continued elaborating their conspiracy. It had been for the purpose of Galen's experiment that the bulls Espartaco faced were drugged. The matador had sought Galen's help to conquer his fears, but he had no idea what had been done to the bulls he fought. Galen wanted to see if Espartaco would become convinced of his invincibility and grow fearless. The fact that his co-conspirators could make money from the knowledge the fights were fixed helped Galen finance his perverse psychological work. And now it was time for him to see how Espartaco faced a bull no longer made docile by drugs. Now it was time to see if the courage the bullfighter had developed over the last few months, falsely based though it was, would be real enough for him to claim a true victory.

I felt a shiver of fear as the story unfolded. I saw a ferocious bull in my mind, heard its fierce snorting, saw its taut muscles and sensed its focused anger and brittle temper. I imagined Espartaco parading towards the animal filled with misplaced boldness and convinced of his invincibility, and shivered again. This time the chill travelled up through my whole body, capturing Galen's attention.

'I hope you did not speak, Syra my pet?'

I shook my head and smiled, pleased by his renewed interest in me.

'Your Syra smiles, Galen,' Gonzalo observed. 'I hope she takes your instructions seriously.'

I smiled again as a thrill of expectation ran through me. I pressed my thighs together and the seam at the crotch of my leggings pulled insistently up into my pussy. I squeezed my buttocks to bear down on the seam, and felt the moist lips of my labia parting around the pressure.

Galen scowled at me, just as two female dancers with long black hair ran onto the stage. Their red and black skirts were parted up the front in a swathe of heavy, oyster-lipped frills, and their bodices were laced tightly over their ample breasts and held closed with shiny black buttons. They pranced to the front of the small stage like horses, clapping their hands in front of their faces, stamping their feet and turning like ponies caught at the limits of a leash, shouting in breathy voices. They picked up the fronts of their skirts and revealed their knees for a teasing instant, leaving only an image in the mind of slender legs. They stood back-to-back pressing their bare shoulders together, leaning on each other, clapping and stamping in a frenzy of unbridled excitement. My ears filling with the rhythmic din, I stretched my legs out further beneath the table and touched Juan Carlos's knee.

I looked at him. He was staring at the dancers, enthralled. I laid my hand on his knee, but he did not respond. I squeezed his thigh and he shuffled his leg slightly, but he still did not look away from the captivating performance. I nodded to him as though he was looking at me, and lowered my gaze modestly as I curled my hand around the top of his thigh, nearer his crotch. I stretched my gloved fingers out and moulded them around the shape of his fleshy cock through his trousers. I felt the roundness of his heavy balls as I cupped them in my hand, holding them more and more firmly until I was squeezing them. His testicles filled my hand and I felt their warmth, even through his slacks and the thin material of my gloves. Lying beside his balls was the thick length of his cock, and when I pressed my fingers against it I could feel it throbbing, waiting like a sleeping monster. It grew in my palm, swelling beneath my light touch. I stroked it, pinching the material containing it, pulling his trousers away from his body and easing a space for his pulsing member to swell to its full length.

The dancers stood at the front of the stage and stamped their feet swiftly and fiercely, almost as if enraged. The audience was caught up in their frenzy as they clapped frantically and mimicked the music with their melodic shouts. I unzipped Juan Carlos's trousers and eased out his rigid penis. I slid my gloved hand along it and felt the bulging veins pulsating on its surface. I caressed the swollen end, feeling around its flared edges and sensing the subtly penetrating heat emanating from it. I could not hold back; I clasped it tightly in my hand and felt the rush of blood within it. I squeezed it more firmly and imagined I could see it beating beneath the strain of my grip. I felt it hardening even more and swelling at the tip as he lifted his hips slightly and climaxed in my grip. I held him as semen poured in a stream onto my gloved palm, hot and sticky, and I did not let go until I was sure I had wrung every last drop of pleasure from him.

I wanted to get underneath the table and lick up his cum. I wanted to crawl on my hands and knees and suck Gonzalo down next, but I knew Galen would be angry if he even suspected what I was thinking. Keeping it carefully cupped, I withdrew my hand from around Juan Carlos's cock, and looking at Galen to make sure his attention was still riveted on the stage, I lifted my hand to my mouth and drank. I lapped up the man's hot semen, tasting its saltiness and feasting on its abundant richness, swallowing it down as though I was a thirsty pilgrim lost in the desert. I closed my eyes and let the viscous liquid slip down my throat, and then, amidst the din of the dancing and the deep tingling in my pussy from the pressure of the leggings digging into my labia, I shuddered in the throes of an orgasm it took all my self-control to conceal. It came suddenly, seemingly out of nowhere, and I dropped my eyes as it coursed through me like a thousand electrifying jolts bursting between my legs and rushing in a blazing current beneath my skin. My nerves were charged as if with lightning, and bolts of pure pleasure shook me to the core as I lapped my sticky palm like a hungry animal.

It was not a word, it was more a gasp, an exhalation, a breathless exclamation of released energy, but it was a sound. I had broken my silence and I knew it. Galen looked at me angrily. He did not say anything, but I could tell he knew exactly what had happened. It was incredibly foolish of me to believe I could deceive him. Even when his attention did not seem to be focused on me, I knew he was aware of me, perhaps even more so than when he was actually looking at me. Everything with this man was a test, and I kept failing miserably. He grabbed my arm, pulled me to my feet and bundled me out of the club. I wanted to say I was sorry, but I said nothing at all - I did not dare.

I did not know what the penalty for disobedience and infidelity would be. I knew there had to be a penalty, a punishment - I would not have been satisfied if there had not been - but I could not imagine what form it would take. Already it was not enough for me to feel guilt and shame for failing to follow instructions, I also needed the deeper humiliation that came with the execution of an appropriate punishment.

Back at his house I sat where he told me to, on the raised platform in the middle of the upper floor, anxiously studying the shiny chromium plated padlock on the hatch. I sensed again that there was something ominous beneath the tight-fitting wooden doors.

'As punishment for your disobedience,' Galen addressed me in the deep, disapproving tone of a judge passing sentence, 'you must sit here for the rest of the night and not speak.'

I felt a sense of relief mingled with disappointment. It was not a cruel enough punishment for my transgression and I felt frustrated and cheated. Surely someone who had been so faithless deserved a much more severe penance.

'However,' he continued, 'I cannot trust you, can I, Syra? You failed before, so this time I will make *sure* you do not speak.' He fetched two chopsticks and placed them horizontally across my mouth, one above my upper lip and the other below my bottom lip. He pinched them together, squeezing my mouth out like a bill, and then tied the ends with a thin cord. I sat with my back stiff and did not move as he applied the ingeniously painful gag.

'As you sit, Syra my pet,' he spoke softly in my ear, 'you can remember drinking Juan Carlos's semen and the pain across your bottom, which will throb all night and remind you that you did not have my permission to act as you did. You may nod if you understand.'

I nodded slowly, and as the tension in the chopsticks tightened, my lips began stinging. I felt tears in the corners of my eyes, but did not dare blink in case it annoyed him. I remained still, my back rigid, my eyes wide open, but I was ready to move the moment he commanded me to. I waited, not daring to glance behind me as he took something out of a drawer in the cabinet. I expected to be told to get on all fours, or to stand and bend over, or to spread myself across his knee, but suddenly I felt the caress of a leather belt across my back and knew I was not to be spanked this time, but thrashed.

'Stand up and remove your dress,' he commanded.

I obeyed at once, flinging the garment away carelessly as I tightened my shoulders against the burning pain that immediately cut across my naked back. He paused, and I realised he was looking at me, waiting to see if I moved or if I remained obediently still. Then another searing blow fell where the first one had already left its smouldering mark. I held myself rigid, my eyes opening even wider as I absorbed the blazing agony, hoping my efforts would please him. The belt struck again, this time further down my back just below my shoulder blades, and for some reason it was harder to bear then the first two lashes. I felt tears welling in my eyes as I struggled to remain motionless. There was a pause - I knew he was watching me again carefully, analysing my reaction - then he brought the belt down on top of the smouldering mark the last blow had burned across my skin.

Tears flowed down my face as the belt kept stroking me cruelly, sometimes with a rhythm I could brace myself against, sometimes at random, with long, indeterminate pauses in between lashes that threw me into a frenzy of dread and anticipation. The last cruel kiss of the leather landed across the top of my buttocks, slapping against them, absorbing the perspiration glistening on my skin so each successive lash sounded louder than the last. My nipples were harder than they had ever been and the heat in my cunt was almost unbearable. I wanted to sink my fingers into it, to feel and relish its softness, cupping my hand against its wetness, but I could not, and it frustrated me terribly even as it heightened my arousal to the point where I must have passed out from the intensity of my lust, which was consuming not only my body but my very soul...

I awoke in what felt like the middle of the night, wracked with pain. I tried to feel my back, but discovered my hands had been tied together over my stomach by a thin rope wrapped around my waist. In order to distract myself, I imagined I heard the slow wash of water beneath me. It made me think of the surface of the sea slowly being broken by a heavy, lazy whale... I imagined the hatchway in the raised platform leading down into the dark centre of a water-filled cave, a place where there was no sensation except the knowledge of being entombed in darkness. I pictured what it was like to be there, drifting serenely in a sense-deprived silence punctuated only by the occasional soft lapping of a wave against an unseen shore.

Later - I think it was later - I saw myself sitting at Galen's feet, asking him what lay beneath the platform, and heard his voice murmuring in my mind, 'Everything you have ever desired, Syra my pet, everything you have ever desired...

CHAPTER 7

For a while I could sense nothing, all my feelings were locked inside me, but now everything is there again, every smell, every taste, every pain, every expectation, every hope, every wish and every desire. It is the world providing me with sensations once more. I wonder if he knows that my sense of being has returned. I wonder if he realises I do not need any more treatment. I wonder whether he understands I have been cured of my terrible ailment. I need to show him what has happened, that I am better again, but every time he comes I simply present what I have written to him, and wait. It is as though I no longer have any will of my own, as though, like everything else, it has been taken from me.

Of course, he is right to ignore my silent pleas, for I have not truly been cured, I know that. Even so, as I write my story I am increasingly embarrassed to think that such a short time ago I was incredibly naive and foolish. Surely this feeling is a good sign and part of my cure.

But the feeling hardly lasts long enough for me to notice, let alone for anyone else to observe, and everything I am writing down only reminds me of the pleasure, the dark delight, the wicked ecstasy of my time with Galen. How can I think of anything other than that perversely beautiful experience? And how can I imagine that a cure for how I felt when I was with him is in itself nothing but a different kind of sickness?

Galen came to me before sunrise. I was sitting up again with my back rigid, staring straight ahead of me with the chopsticks tied across my lips, and I did not turn towards him as I heard him approaching. He undid the thin twine at the ends of the chopsticks, and looked at me for a while before he finally released my hands. I remained sitting impassively, not moving, not rubbing my aching limbs nor exercising my stiff lips. I stared straight ahead as if seeing right into eternity.

Suddenly I shivered uncontrollably and immediately felt guilty about having moved. I could still feel the constricting chopsticks across my lips, even though they were no longer there. When he first tied them across my mouth I experienced the pain that accompanied the pinching pressure. It tormented me for hours after I awoke alone in the dark, and then my lips went mercifully numb. They were tingling terribly now as the blood rushed back into them and sensation gradually returned.

'Go and sleep some more now, my pet,' he said gently. 'On a nice comfortable bed with no bondage constricting you.'

I got up, moaning softly. My whole body felt stiff and my back was still aching from his beating. I walked to the bedroom, lay on the bed as he had instructed, and fell swiftly into a deep and dreamless sleep.

I sat up, startled by a hand shaking my sore shoulders. The hand belonged to Eve. She had a white towel draped across her shoulders and was dripping wet. Her dark hair hung in snakelike coils over her shoulders and her tanned skin shimmered like a mermaid's beneath her strangely glazed eyes. She was sitting on the edge of the bed, looking directly at my naked pussy. I pulled my legs together a little, in a hopeless attempt to ease the nervous thrill surging through me as I gazed at the pert swell of her breasts beneath the wet towel. My feelings were an oncoming storm flashing with sparks of energy building up inside me. My eyes glazed as I found it hard to focus, feeling the tingling onset of an orgasm wanting to happen. I bit my lip to try and suppress it, but the pain where the chopsticks had been - a jolting reminder of my night of captivity - was like a plug being pulled and releasing the pent-up wave of ecstasy that flowed now unstoppable. I gasped and sat up slightly as the pleasure crested directly between my legs, and then fell back across the mattress as if flung there. The

52

climax drained slowly out of me in my pussy juices, exhausting me, sapping my vitality and leaving me completely depleted. I stared up at the ceiling not remembering for a moment where I was, my thoughts in complete disarray...

The next thing I knew Eve was shaking me again, this time more urgently, as though my awaking would help snap the vague look out of her own dark eyes. Rising after her, I followed her lethargic steps to the upstairs floor and once more seated myself on the raised platform. I glanced down, and saw the padlock was not in its place securing the hasp and staple over the trapdoor. I watched her move out onto the balcony and drop the towel to the floor. She stood naked near the edge, lazily caressing her breasts in the sunshine. She circled them with the tips of her fingers, and then squeezed her erect nipples as if trying to pinch herself fully awake. She looked like the statue of a goddess, golden-skinned, perfectly formed and glistening with divine nectar. It was as if the gods themselves had anointed her in preparation for licking the ambrosial drops from her succulent body, as though without this sweet moisture on their tongues their eternal lives were meaningless. She stepped sideways, standing between me and the sun, and a blazing halo of light formed around her body as though she was burning with a force beyond the understanding of mere mortals.

Absently, I lifted the metal hasp sitting unprotected beside the padlock, the shiny staple bent in a hook within the hole at its end. It came free easily, and when I tugged at it a little more, the crack between the tight-fitting doors of the hatch opened slightly, enabling me to look inside. A steel bar was fixed beneath the crack and at its centre sat a reel like a small windlass. I bent forward to stare beyond it, but saw only darkness. I opened the door wider, lifting until it was at a right angle to the top of the rostrum, but still I could see nothing. It was completely black inside - a silent, abysmal void. I felt disappointed and angry, remembering Galen's proclamation that beneath the hinged doors lay 'everything I had ever desired'. There was nothing there; his promise was empty and I pouted in profound annoyance.

He entered the room suddenly and called Eve off the balcony. He asked her if she was all right, and she nodded, unconvincingly, I thought. 'Perhaps it was too much for you?' he asked cryptically.

'Never,' she said firmly, blinking hard, as though having stared at the sun for so long she could not rid herself of the silhouette blotting out her vision.

He came to me and draped his arm around my shoulders. 'Syra, my pet, are you ready to pursue your goal? Are you prepared to approach your fears and awaken your darkest sexual desires? Are you, as you agreed, ready to be truly bad?'

The question seemed loaded with menace and I felt confused. The way forward seemed to have no limits, no restrictions, and I shivered at the thought of what awaited me, but I could not go back, of that I was sure. 'Please,' I whispered, as if my will was indistinguishable from his, 'take me to the limit.'

This time he told me I must wear a vest, a skirt and sandals and nothing else, but I could choose them from the closet myself. I showered, and then selected a tight white vest, a short black pleated skirt and black leather sandals with shiny metal buckles. The skirt fitted tightly around my hips and the pleats spun out when I turned around swiftly. Galen seemed pleased when I presented myself to him. He told me to bend over and touch my toes. He wanted to determine how far he could see up my skirt. I obeyed him and waited while he stared at me. I knew what he could see and I felt moisture collecting between the exposed lips of my pussy.

The same taxi driver as before picked us up and drove us to the bullring again. Eve sat in the front and I sat in the back beside Galen. The dark-haired driver leered at me in the rear-view mirror, but I pretended to ignore him. He tilted the mirror down and I could tell he was attempting to look up my skirt. I did not ask for Galen's approval - I chose to believe I had it - and opened my legs enough for the young man to glimpse the pouting lips of my delectable slit. He adjusted the mirror again and I moved forward slightly on the seat so I could spread my legs just a little bit more.

The sensation of his gaze focused alternately on the road and on my naked sex was like being stroked with something soft and smooth, and yet at the same time slightly and excitingly abrasive. I felt his penetrating glances mysteriously parting my labia and prying into the darker pink folds leading into my vagina. His eyes found my clitoris, and as I squeezed my buttocks together and edged forward in the seat even more, I felt his stare pressing against its inflamed tip. I wanted to lift my skirt around my waist and drape myself over the front seat, bent at the waist, my naked bottom thrust high and visible through the windows as I took his cock in my mouth and sucked him down while he drove through the busy streets. I pictured the gawking stares of passers-by as I lowered my face over his throbbing erection, letting my weight drive it deep into my mouth until it filled the back of my throat. I imagined the cab stopped at a busy intersection and faces peering through the windows, staring at me as I swallowed his pulsating flesh, gulping it down greedily, consuming it and nearly drowning myself in the salty fountain that erupted into my throat...

Galen reached over and pulled the hem of my skirt down. The pleats dipped between my knees and completely covered my pussy. I felt censured from my own fantasies and stupid for assuming he did not know my thoughts. I dropped my gaze and pressed the pleats firmly between my thighs to protect what lay beneath them from the driver's gaze.

Galen paid the man and told him to wait; we would not be more than an hour, he said. He held my arm as we walked through the entrance tunnel while Eve walked behind us listlessly, a loose-fitting red leather jacket hanging from her shoulders and a short white skirt riding high up her thighs with her every step. Mora was in the president's box, and when he saw us step out onto the terraces, he waved and beckoned to us enthusiastically.

'No Espartaco today,' he declared, as we entered the red-curtained box. 'Perhaps he has lost his courage and run away.'

Galen patted the chair next to his and I sat down. The pet did not join us in the box, but wandered off into the crowd, pulling her jacket back onto her shoulders

54

whenever it was inadvertently knocked off by the glancing caress of someone she brushed past. Galen talked to Mora about Espartaco. He told him the agreement he had come to with Gonzalo and Juan Carlos, and they laughed together about the matador's fate.

'You will see, Mora, Espartaco will be my greatest success yet,' Galen concluded arrogantly, and then looked at me. 'Although there may be greater successes in the future,' he added, smiling.

I nodded at him silently, thrilled by his words but concealing my pleasure.

'Look,' Mora said, 'there is Juan Carlos now. He has a young woman with him. Perhaps he has brought you someone fresh for your experiments? Perhaps *she* will be the next subject of your research? Yes, perhaps she will be the success that will eclipse all your other achievements, including Espartaco.'

Juan Carlos pushed his way across the terrace towards the box. Behind him trailed the young blonde with the short dress I had seen him watching yesterday. She looked innocent and energetic as she hung onto his outstretched hand and stepped through the crowd. She wore a wide-brimmed straw hat and her long hair hung across her shoulders from beneath it. Her pale skin seemed to shine in the dappled illumination pouring in from beneath the latticework of the hat, covering her in gentle flickering lights, accentuating her youth and vitality.

'I have brought someone to meet you,' Juan Carlos announced, sounding slightly out of breath.

'So I see,' Galen replied serenely. 'You remember my pet, Syra, I'm sure.'

Juan Carlos looked a bit embarrassed. He nodded vaguely in my direction, the polite way he inclined his head expressing a weight of guilt along with an acknowledgement of our secret, which he obviously hoped was still safe.

I nodded back at him and smiled, but my smile did not bless our complicity, it was an expression of pleasure as I was reminded of the delectable pain I had suffered for my faithless disobedience with him.

'You *do* remember my pet, Syra, don't you?' Galen asked him again.

'*Si, si...* yes, of course,' he said, apparently flustered.

'And who is *your* new acquaintance?' Galen had not taken his eyes off the young blonde since she'd entered the box.

She extended her arm without being introduced, and her pert breasts were outlined against her pale cream dress as Galen took her hand, seemingly captivated by her air of naive enthusiasm. She sat down next to him and I observed that her legs were beautifully shaped and firm with youth. She turned her face towards his. 'Juan says you are on the lookout for students to take part in your experiments,' she spoke with an American accent. 'I'm Cleo, Cleo Gresham, and I'm really keen to take part in them, Mr Galen. I assume you pay?'

He smiled at her, and then laughed, delighted. Her bluntness amused him and he revelled in the closeness of her nubile young body. 'Yes I do, Cleo, if you perform well.'

'Then look no further!' she exclaimed. 'Take me to your laboratory!'

'Slow down, slow down,' Galen urged her, still chuckling. 'Juan Carlos will bring you to my house later. We can sort things out there.'

We sat through several bullfights. I was not so keen on watching the bloody display as I had been yesterday when Espartaco was in the arena. I was more interested in Cleo and the way she was fawning over Galen. She rested her hand on his knee, pressing down on it as she feigned to concentrate on what he was saying, because her slightly vacant gaze told me she was not really listening. When there was a gap in the conversation she filled it with some inane comment, and I came to the catty conclusion that she was not very bright. Her energy was initially engaging, but as the sun began descending from its burning throne at the sky's zenith, Galen seemed to begin tiring of her.

The last match of the afternoon was disappointing. The bull would not fight and the matador circled the ring in apologetic frustration, looking lonely as he paraded his loss and depression before the unresponsive crowd. Then Galen announced he wanted to go look at some of the bulls.

We walked around a network of corrals located below the stadium, and several young bulls thrashed restlessly against the sides of their pens as we approached.

'They are like you, Cleo,' Galen remarked, 'very lively.'

She pushed her hat off, and the string dangling from each side of the wide brim pressed against her throat as the weight of the straw fell between her shoulder blades. She jumped up on the side of a heavily built pen and reached out to the bull pacing around inside it. Her short dress hiked up as she bent forward, revealing a pair of tight white panties riding up into the cleft of her firm buttocks.

'Why is this one blindfolded?' she asked curiously, leaning over further and extending one shapely leg for balance.

'So he cannot see your panties and go mad with lust,' Galen replied, smiling.

She ignored his compliment and leaned even further over the edge of the pen, exposing the tight bulge of her pudenda inside the taut material of her panties. 'You really are a sweetie,' she cooed, caressing the bull's ears and tickling his nose while he stood perfectly still, as though astonished someone was daring to touch him so casually. 'Such a little angel you are, and they won't allow you to see anything,' she murmured, stroking his muzzle. 'There, there...'

I was amazed by her complete lack of fear, or she was incredibly stupid and did not realise the danger she was in. She was treating this wild creature like a domesticated pet. I wanted to jump up beside her and show Galen I was as fearless as she was, but it seemed a ridiculous gesture, stupidly competitive, an act of rivalry unworthy of me, so I did nothing.

We walked to the place where the bulls were released into the ring. A heavily built barrier of horizontal timbers barred the way, and when the bull entered the arena from the pens below it forced him sideways, disorienting him before he caught sight of his waiting foe. A heavily tooled black leather saddle sat on top of the wooden barrier, and Eve was leaning on one end of it talking to a young man wearing jeans and brown leather chaps tied over them with leather thongs. The worn and shiny chaps were cut off halfway up his thighs, and because they were pulled up and tied on the outside of his hips to his belt, they accentuated

56

the already large bulge at his crotch.

Galen walked over to the pet, and cupping her breasts, kissed her passionately on the mouth. She returned his kiss fervently, placing her hands firmly against the nape of his neck and pressing her body tightly against his as she raised herself up onto her toes. I could see she was thrusting her tongue deeply into his mouth, and wanted to snatch her away from him and take her place.

Cleo rushed past me and walked straight up to the young man. She boldly stroked the shiny leather of his riding chaps with both hands, and they laughed like old lovers. I hated her in that moment, hated her easy intimacy and her fearlessness. It was what Galen had promised for me, and it was as if with every one of her precocious actions she was stealing away my own fate.

Galen finally released Eve and she stepped back away from him, caressing her forehead as though dizzy and trying to focus.

'My students have to pass an entrance test,' Galen stated.

'Then I will take it!' Cleo cried and stood at attention, her back rigid and her chin thrust into the air.

'Your test is simple,' he told her.

'Yes?' she insisted, obviously eager to prove she could easily pass with flying colours.

'To give me pleasure.'

'Oh, that *will* be easy,' she said, pressing the tip of her forefinger against her nose as she pretended to consider the problem.

'But, of course, as with any test, you have competitors.' Galen extended his hand, first towards Eve and then towards me.

I felt annoyed at being used like this, as a prop, and I hated Cleo for invading the springtime of my new world with Galen. I wanted to call her names and grab her by the hair and toss her out of the arena. I wanted to incite the crowd to jeer at her and show Galen what a fool she was. But I suppressed my jealous rage. Surely he could not have abandoned me so quickly. It was impossible he had given up on me without testing me further. His experiment with me had only just begun and already I knew he was not the kind of man to give up so easily. He looked at me, and held my eyes as if I should be able to understand his thoughts, as if there was some secret communion between us, but I could only stare back at him morosely, my mind filled with the apathy of a forsaken and jealous lover.

He instructed us to stand with our backs against the wooden barrier, and the three of us did as we were told. We stood in a row almost touching each other, with Cleo in the centre, watching as he gathered some red ribbons from a bunch hanging next to the bull pens, and handed them to the man with the leather riding chaps. Without being instructed, he walked up to Cleo and placed one of the ribbons over her eyes, wrapping it around her head and effectively blindfolding her. She did not speak, but I could see by the way she squeezed her thighs together that she was excited. He then attempted to blindfold Eve, but she pushed his hand away and looked at Galen as if unprepared to submit to anyone or anything without a direct order from him. He nodded, and she immediately closed her eyes as the ribbon was tied tightly around her head.

The young man then stood in front of me with ribbons dangling from his hand, and I wondered what I should do. Should I submit like Cleo, squeezing my knees together in excited anticipation, or should I surrender impassively like Eve as if nothing in the world could harm me? He held up the ribbon and I pushed it away.

'Is your wickedness still in sight, Syra?' Galen enquired sternly.

'Yes,' I replied, 'it is.'

'Then why do you resist? You have nothing to fear. I will be watching you, my pet.'

I felt my insides melting, as if my soul had been snowbound and now, magically transported to a tropical shore, I was swiftly thawing out in the generous warmth of the sun. I felt myself basking in his words and the tenderness in his voice. He would be watching me. What more could I wish for? I tilted my head back slightly and parted my lips as I yielded to the red ribbon.

I heard nothing to begin with; everything was silent. Then, after a few moments, I began to hear the buzz of insects coming and going as they hurried along seemingly erratic but actually purposeful routes. I turned my head to one side to follow their progress, but stiffened suddenly as I heard someone walking up in front of me. I lifted my head slightly and cocked it to one side, waiting for a clue as to whose footsteps they were. Then I heard Eve moan... or was it Cleo? I could not tell. The sound came again, a low purring noise but smoother, like a deeply satisfied sigh. I cocked my head again and concentrated... it *was* Eve moaning, I was sure of it.

I imagined Galen watching me as the young man in the leather chaps stood in front of the pet. Yes, Galen would not be interested in her, he had told me he was going to be watching me, I was all that mattered to him. A surge of pleasure coursed through me at the thought. I was blindfolded, unable to know what he was planning for me, unable to see what was happening around me, but all the time he would be watching only me...

I heard the moaning sound again. This time it broke off in the middle, and I imagined the young man stroking Eve's pussy with the flat of his hand, making it wet, teasing her labia with his fingers, prising open the soft petals and exposing the darker inner flesh before suddenly finding her clitoris with his fingertips. But had he taken her panties off? I was not even sure she was wearing panties. If she was, perhaps he simply edged the gusset aside so he could touch her naked flesh...

This time I heard a gasp as though she was restraining an orgasm, trying to hold it back, waiting until she was given permission to release it. She gasped again, a soft inhalation of breath, and then was silent, as though biting her lip to keep from crying out. I listened intently, and heard what sounded like skin brushing against something - something smooth and supple. Yes, she was pulling her legs up around the man's shiny leather riding chaps, delighting in the feel of her flesh against them and allowing it to feed her passion. I heard a soft but distinct cry and the motion of her legs against the leather increased in pace.

The caressing was more rapid, more urgent, more in need of satisfaction, and her next moan was less restrained, an open admission of passion breaking free inside her. I listened to the subtle whispers of their limbs intertwining. I seemed to be able to hear him driving his hips against hers, rubbing the leather against the insides of her thighs, massaging her, stroking her. I wondered if she was riding him, her arms wrapped around his neck, her legs around his hips. Was she impaling herself on him in a frenzy of lust, clawing at him, digging her nails into his neck?

I could sense her feeling the heat from his body, tasting his lips as she rode his erection. Did I hear his trousers being undone? Did I hear him opening them and releasing his fleshy cock, holding the rigid offering in his hands, feeling its throbbing veins and pulsating centre? Was she wrapping her legs even more tightly around his hips now? I heard her panting, breathing hard, forcing herself down over him, forcing him deeper and deeper inside her. Then there was a moment of sudden stillness and silence, a second of inactivity just before I imagined them climaxing together explosively, his semen bubbling into her as her vaginal muscles clenched around him. And in that moment of expectation, that breathless pause before a deluge of delights, I heard another equally urgent and rhythmic gasping, the sound of someone reaching her own delectable fulfilment. The panting breaths were accompanied by a sense of movement, and I pictured Cleo masturbating as she listened to Eve being fucked, and Galen watching her. He was seeing her with her white panties pulled down around her knees, the red blindfold across her eyes, her dress pulled up above her firm breasts. He was watching her hand where it was working between her legs, teasing the flesh of her labia, playing with the soft folds and releasing the magical energy contained in the hard clitoris crowning them. In my mind's eye I could see her as clearly as Galen could, a nubile young beauty lost in her own world of pleasure and energised by it, her senses reeling with whatever erotic images aroused her most as she played with herself, enjoying her body and holding back only as long as she wanted to, until she knew he had seen enough and could release her blinding orgasm.

I did not know what to do. I did not know whether to sink to my knees and crawl towards him, to show how readily I could submit, to show I did not care what happened to me as long as he was there and watching *me*. I wanted to beg him to have me tied to the barrier and left there until the crowds returned. I wanted to plead with him to tie me against the saddle slung across the top of the barrier and make me wait until the first raging bull - froth spilling from its mouth as it shook its heavy head - charged from the pen and stopped in front of me, confused, not knowing which way to turn. My thoughts were trampled by a muddled turmoil of emotions, but I knew I had to show him, had to prove to him I was worth watching...

I stepped forward, but hands gripped my wrists and lifted my arms. I was forced back against the heavy boarded barrier and my outstretched wrists were tied against it. I thought of struggling, perhaps that was what he wanted, to watch me fighting for my freedom, but before I could decide how to react I felt smooth leather pressing against the insides of my bare thighs as my skirt was eased up around my waist, and the unmistakable warmth of a throbbing cock pressed against the wet folds of my moist cunt.

I cannot say what I felt most as the anonymous erection thrust up inside me. My ears were still filled with moaning sounds of struggle and delight, my mind was crammed with images of perspiring bodies shuddering in the throes of ecstasy, and my pussy was filled with a rigid, unyielding heat lifting me up around it as though I was being impaled on a freshly forged iron rod. I was so weak with lust I could only allow myself to be taken, my hands held fast above my head, my back forced against the rough planks of the barrier and my mind spinning with a dazzling kaleidoscope of sensual images. I felt as if I might not survive the exquisite tumult, as if there was nothing to hold on to except the cock inside me, and even though it hurt not knowing whom it belonged to, its thrusting energy was also my only hope. Its rigid length pinned me against the wall and held me fast, opening me up as it forced and pumped its way in and out of me, faster and harder. My pussy clung to it, tightening around its pulsing length, and when finally, moaning and gasping, I was overtaken by a convulsive climax, I screamed like an animal skewered on a spear.

I do not recall being untied or taken down from the barrier like a victim from a cross. I do not remember the large cock slipping out of me and I do not remember the perspiring breathlessness of recovering from its excruciatingly pleasurable invasion. But I do remember the blindfold being torn off and the dazzling flood of light.

To my delight, Cleo left with Juan Carlos and Eve said she wanted to stay at the bullring for a while, so I was alone with Galen as he walked with me back to the waiting cab.

'I will drive,' he said to the taxi driver, who did not look surprised by the curt statement. 'You get in the back with the girl. I want you to fuck her. She does not have any panties on, so you will need to find something else to tie her wrists with.' He slipped into the front and started the engine.

I lay across the back seat as the driver got in beside me. The taxi pulled away from the curb with a jolt, and then Galen rested his arm on the back of the seat as he told the young man what to do with me, how to fuck me, how to use me.

I shivered with excitement, listening to him without really hearing his words, my head reeling as he issued detailed instructions - how tightly I was to be restricted and how roughly, and in what order I was to be undressed, how swiftly I was to be penetrated, and how fast and how hard he should thrust his cock into me in order to delay my orgasm. I wanted to hear more. I wanted to hear his description of how I should be made to lie, my exact position, whether I should be allowed to move, even slightly, and make any noise, or whether I should be perfectly still and silent. I wanted to hear him tell the driver where exactly he should come inside me. And if he was not to come inside me, I wanted my master to tell him where to ejaculate and whether he should rub it into my breasts, let it jet across my stomach or between my wet thighs, or whether I should take it all in my mouth and swallow every last drop. And, of course, I wanted to know he was going to watch it all. I wanted to know my master would be looking at me the whole time to ensure we both did everything right. Because if I did not do everything right, then I had to be punished...

The driver put his hands on my thighs and spread my legs wide. My naked pussy was fully exposed to him, pink and moist and glistening at the centre. I could still hear Galen talking to him, but it was harder now to make out his words as the young man lifted my knees and knelt between my legs. I looked up at him, waiting for him to do Galen's bidding.

He stared down at me a moment before taking hold of my wrists and securing them inside the leather loop hanging above the door. It pinched my skin and I gasped in discomfort as he twisted the strap painfully tight. Then he took hold of my left ankle and slipped my foot into the strap on the opposite side of the car, leaving me stretched out with my arms pulled up on one side and one leg drawn up on the other.

I heard Galen telling him to undo his trousers and twisted my hips slightly - my master had not ordered me to be still - and felt moisture running freely at the centre of my vulnerable pussy. I felt a touch of heat, a subtle burning as the tip of his erection touched me. The soft petals of my labia opened to receive it, parting slowly and expanding around its girth as it slipped inside me. The veins on its surface beat against my delicate flesh, pulsating rhythmically and sending me into a strange, nervous trance. I could still hear Galen's words as though he was a conductor orchestrating our every movement, every thrust, every tightening of the bonds at my wrists and ankle. But then even his commands were lost to me, swallowed up by the shivers of ecstasy coursing through my body and flooding my mind. I was mesmerised, caught up in a bizarre dream, as if the real world had been suspended and I was living out some kind of half-waking reverie.

The young driver rammed into me roughly, angrily. His hips grazed against the insides of my thighs as he shoved his cock as deep inside me as he possibly could. Every jolt of the cab buried him even deeper between my legs as his rigid penis swelled and pulsed in time with his hands squeezing my buttocks. He dug his fingers into my tender flesh, holding my left cheek as hard as he could, bracing himself on it as he pounded into me.

Then he began spanking me with his other hand, and my right buttock burned beneath every smack of his open palm as his frenzy increased and the force and pace of his blows intensified. My pussy was fully stretched around him, and I felt as though I would die from the terrible pleasure as he erupted inside me with a prolonged burst of hot spunk that seemed to scald my insides. He spanked me a few more times as the last drops of semen trickled from his engorged glans, but the blows were not so fierce and I was so sore I could hardly feel them any more.

Then, suddenly, he twisted me sideways, shoved his knee beneath my hip, and started spanking me again with renewed fervour. I cried out in pain and climaxed violently as the flat of his hand kept beating relentlessly down on my burning bottom.

I must stop writing now. I suffered the impression suddenly that what I was setting down on paper would not please him, and now I cannot go on. I do not know what I can do though, for it is all the truth and he told me I must only write exactly what happened and exactly how I felt. Nevertheless, I feel he will not like what I have said and I am paralysed by fear and indecision.

Chapter 8

This time when I handed him my work he smiled as though what he read pleased him. I did not trust him, however, so I did not smile back in case he was making an effort to trick me into believing he approved of my efforts. I was still concerned I had been doing wrong, that my story was not what he wanted from me. I waited impatiently, and yet seemingly quite patiently, while he read. I sat up straight even though he did not tell me to, and I did not move because I thought my being still would placate any anger my words might inspire in him. I could not stop myself worrying about what he might say and the nervous clenching of my stomach, for I had used the word *cunt* again, and more than once.

Finally, he set the pages down on the floor and asked me if I wanted to suck him. I was not sure what to say or do. It seemed impossible for me to make a decision. Why had he not just commanded me to suck me? I felt ashamed that I had believed myself cured. How could I be better if I could not decide how to answer him?

Suddenly, without thinking, as though being mindless was the only way of effectively directing my actions, I dropped onto all fours and pressed my face clumsily against his groin. I struggled to undo his trousers, panicking because they would not come undone, but as I took hold of his cock and started licking his cool glans, he pulled himself away abruptly and stood up.

As he left he shook his head in despair and I felt he was condemning me as a lost cause, as hopeless and beyond redemption, and I knew I had failed again. I should have shown him I could resist. Of course, that was what he was checking to see, what he was trying to find out, if I could hold back, and I had failed the test dismally. I hoped he would not give up on me. I prayed he would not abandon me, not now, not after all I had been through, not after I had come this far.

I waited for him to return, sitting up straight against the wall beside the door, trying to please him even though he could not see me. I thought that when he came back and found me there he would be pleased with me and would let me suck him, not as a test but as a reward for my good behaviour.

When he finally did return, he brought extra paper and some fresh pencils. He placed them at the opposite corner of the room away from the door, and told me to start working again straightaway, and not stop until he returned again. I crawled across the floor on my hands and knees as he stood by the door watching me, and when he closed it, I huddled in the corner and began writing again.

I was dozing, and woke up with a start when the taxi driver opened the door the next morning. It had not been locked. I do not remember when Galen left, when either of them left, all I know is I was alone all night, tied up in an unlocked cab parked in a dimly lit district of the city, at the mercy of anyone who happened to pass by and felt like making use of my body. It seemed a miracle no one at all had molested me.

The driver leered in where I hung, still stretched out between the two leather straps, my skirt pulled up around my waist, dried semen glistening on the insides of my thighs. I felt ashamed of my exposed and vulnerable position and tried to bring my free leg up to protect myself from his gaze, but he pushed it down. My arms and leg were numb and my bottom was still throbbing dully from the vicious spanking he had given me. He slipped into the back, knelt between my thighs and unzipped his trousers. I kicked out at him with my free leg and writhed against the seat in an effort to force him away. He sat back, startled by my resistance. He clearly assumed he could take me again, as though we had become lovers. I kicked out at him again, but this time he slipped an arm beneath my hips, lifted my bottom and spanked me hard. I knew it was punishment for refusing him, for holding back. and as the stinging pain merged with the aching need in my pussy, I felt my muscles relaxing and went limp to let him know I was ready for him now.

He noticed my capitulation, but did not stop spanking me, swatting his hand down harder with every blow he subjected me to. I bit my lip and waited, knowing he would not stop until he saw the glow of jagged redness produced by a hard and deliberate spanking. Finally he dropped me against the seat, pulled his cock out, leaned over me and forced himself into my mouth. I sucked him, taking him deep between my lips, and as soon as his throbbing tip grazed the back of my throat I felt the surge of his orgasm. I prepared to swallow his seed, but he pulled out of my mouth and sprayed it all over my throat and vest. Then he zipped up his trousers, got out of the taxi again and slammed the door behind him.

I closed my eyes, frightened and excited, wondering what would happen to me next as I imagined a total stranger opening the door and using me...

He slipped into the driver's seat and drove the cab out of the derelict area where it had sat all night with me bound helplessly inside. I felt shy about anyone looking in and seeing me, still tied with my legs spread out across the back seat, my buttocks red from a fresh spanking and my vest damp and sticky with semen. Every corner we turned made my stomach churn with nerves as I dreaded people looking in and gawping and pointing at me. The thought was unbearable.

The cab stopped suddenly at the end of a narrow alley, and leaning out of the window the driver shouted at two men who stood talking beside a dustbin. I shivered as a dark feeling of foreboding welled up inside me. I twisted my

63

wrists frantically against the restraining strap, but it would not loosen; I was held fast.

The two men approached the car, laughing and shoving each other playfully, very much like excited schoolboys. One was taller than the other, and it was he who bent down to speak to the driver. He peered into the back, and saw me still struggling against the straps. For a second I glared, challenging him, and when he reached in through the window and grabbed my ankle I turned my face towards the seat and struggled wildly. But the straps still did not give and my efforts only caused my limbs to ache even more.

The other man leaned down to stare at me through the back window, and I knew I was to be their victim. There was no escape. They would do with me whatever they desired. I pulled against the strap holding my wrists just to feel the tension, just to feel how restrained I was, just to relish the impossibility of freeing myself. I stretched my fingers and twisted my body, writhing like a captive animal slung on a pole borne by natives, the prize of a successful hunt.

The back door opened, and to me it sounded like the creaking of a door to a condemned person's cell. I shivered as I felt a draft of air against my skin and a warm hand touched my free ankle, its fingers wrapping around it and forming a tight, living manacle. I shook my leg, trying to kick the hand away, but its grip only tightened relentlessly. I pressed my face against the seat, bit my lip and kicked again with all my strength. This time I succeeded in breaking the grip of the man holding me, and he actually groaned in pain as my foot sank into some soft part of his anatomy.

I sensed their anger, but also their indecision. They seemed unable to decide just how much force to use against me. They were unsure of themselves, and I took advantage of their weakness to kick again as hard as I could. I heard a curse and felt more of their uncertainty, but also more of their anger. Someone pulled at my ankle hanging from the leather strap, and although my leg flexed and twisted, my ankle stayed fixed firmly in place... until I suddenly felt the strap give slightly.

I was like a prisoner glimpsing a chink of light in the wall of her dark cell; the slight slackening of my bonds suddenly gave me hope. I screwed my eyes shut and kicked with all my strength, gasping and panting from the strain. I kicked frantically, exhausting myself as I heard the men shouting at me and at each other, but I did not feel their hands on me. I stopped struggling for a second to listen as a cornered animal might pause, its heart hammering against its ribs, seconds before it is caught by wolves. I could hear nothing, and then suddenly they pressed my face down against the seat and all I could think about was how they were planning to fuck me, and how often.

My pussy was helplessly exposed, its soft depths utterly open to them, and I felt their hungry eyes on it. I squirmed, but now I did not consider trying to escape. I tensed my muscles against what was coming, but the tightening of my thighs and the pulling together of my buttocks only served to increase the moistening glow of anticipation in my cunt.

The leather strap around my wrists was undone, but immediately my free leg

64

was pulled up with the other one and firmly secured. They lifted my face away from the seat and draped my head and shoulders back over the seat towards the floor of the taxi. I hung suspended on the strap by my ankles, panting and frightened, my head spinning. Rough hands groped my buttocks, feeling their smooth surface and the taut tension below the skin, and then a hand forced itself between my thighs, creating a big enough space to enable another hand to press flat against my pussy. I swallowed my fear as fingers probed me, searching out the conventional entrance to my body before working back and fingering my anus. Then I gasped in pain as a punishing hand fell across my buttocks. One man spanked me as the other knelt on the seat and held his cock down in front of my face. I watched it throbbing as he rubbed it, and as his companion spanked me faster and harder I obediently flicked my tongue out and licked the swollen glans looming over me. I touched the tip of the stranger's erection and felt its heat, tasting the salty tang as it ran like a flood up its length and out through the sensitive rift. I licked it, my tongue keeping breathless time with the spanking hand making my bottom burn unbearably, and as I caught the white wave of sperm cresting out of the pulsing cock pressing against my lips, I felt another rush of viscous liquid running down my bottom cheeks and slipping into their cleft. The man kept spanking me as he came, smacking his open palm against his own sticky semen as it trickled over my buttocks and between my cheeks.

As if in a dream I heard the cab door slam shut, and they were gone. Then the taxi was moving again.

I managed to wriggle my ankles out of the strap and sit up, my head spinning. Miraculously I found a clean tissue on the seat and wiped my sticky face and buttocks with it. I sat up straighter, and winced as contact with the seat stung my aching bottom. I eased my skirt down and sat with my cheek resting against the cool window frame, staring intently out at the world as warm air blew threw my hair. Instead of feeling ashamed, I felt serene and expectant, as if I was being taken somewhere secret and very special on the orders of my mysterious master. I watched the city streets flash by like photographs in an album. I looked at the crowds gathered together in knots outside cafes, I saw tourists holding their cameras to their eyes and lovers embracing with the keenness of new romance. I was intrigued that none of these people knew what was happening to me. All of them were unaware of my daring contract with Galen, of the bargain I had made with him to expose myself to all my fears and risk everything to conquer them and unleash my deepest, darkest desires.

By the time we pulled up outside Galen's house it was very hot. The driver waited for me to get out of the cab, and then led the way, still without deigning to look at me. I felt as though I had misbehaved and was now being taken to my master's lair to be punished. I hung my head, trying to show my shame, and my stomach filled with excited butterflies. I pictured myself as a servant girl being marched to the master's study for a caning. I tugged my skirt down as far as I could as if trying to protect my naked bottom from what I knew it was about to receive, perfectly aware that he would lift my skirt before the punishment began. My flesh tingled with anticipation and I felt the pressure of my hardening nipples against the thin material of my vest.

Galen was standing at the foot of the spiral staircase. The taxi driver walked straight over to him. My master held up his hand, instructing me to wait at a distance. My stomach churned with excitement again as I watched the driver speak to him, directly in his ear. They both looked over at me a couple of times during the brief conversation, and then Galen patted him on the shoulder and pressed some money into his hand. The driver smiled, and without looking at me again, left the house.

Galen slowly ran his fingers through his hair. He pursed his lips as if considering my fate, and his dark eyes were obscured as he narrowed them in pensive consternation. I imagined him wondering how many strokes of the cane to give me, whether I had been sufficiently disobedient to deserve six or whether I should only get four. I looked around to see what he might tell me to bend over, but there was no particularly suitable furniture in sight. Perhaps he would make me bend over and hold my ankles, a position that would make my bottom taut and vulnerable. Or perhaps he would order me onto my hands and knees on the marble bench. The smoothness of the stone would be perfect. I could pull my vest up and bare my breasts and lie across it relishing the cold hardness against my nipples. I would let him pull up my skirt as high as he wanted, and I would feel the thin material folding across my bottom as he bared it in readiness for my deserved punishment. I would tighten my buttocks together so the cane would strike only them, so the delicate flesh of my pussy would be protected, and the firmness of my clenched bottom cheeks would make the strokes land even more painfully. My lips were dry imagining all this, and as I licked them I felt the warmth of my breath as it passed over them in anxious gasps of anticipation.

He approached me, still scratching his head in a theatrical parody of perplexity, which strangely enough struck me as genuine. Perhaps he was not sure what to punish me for, since I had misbehaved so much lately. My resistance back in the cab was a mistake. I knew that now. But I had been taken by surprise then, not realising Galen did not need to be present in order for me to obey him. Yet I did not want to apologise, to wriggle out of my punishment. I wanted to be chastised. I wanted to be caned, to be bent over and painfully humiliated for my behaviour. I wanted the taxi driver to come back and watch me being beaten, and if Galen ordered, I wanted him to also take the cane and thrash me for as long as he wanted to.

My handsome master finally smiled and nodded at me knowingly. 'Syra, my pet, what have you been doing? You have not been doing what you promised me you would. Have you? You have not been truly bad. You have been resisting your wickedness and fearing it, haven't you?'

I wanted to say I was sorry and that it would not happen again. I wanted to tell him I would take my punishment now and do better in the future, but my throat was too dry to enable me to speak.

'I wonder why this is?' he continued, almost as if talking to himself. 'Have you

66

forgotten your contract with me? Surely not.'

I wanted to pull up my vest, bend over the marble bench and take my punishment as I pressed my breasts against the cold stone, but he had not told me to move, so I did not move.

'Answer me, Syra.'

'It was only at first,' I explained quietly, 'because you were not there. I did not want to do anything unless you told me to do it... and you were not there...'

'Syra, my pet, don't you realise yet that I am always there? There is nothing you can do now that I have not instructed you to do.' He sighed dramatically. 'Really, Syra, you can be so innocent. Do you think I would have left you alone by mistake?'

I felt incredibly stupid. Unable to meet his hypnotically dark gaze, I walked towards the bench and looked down at it. I rubbed my hand across my belly, lifting the bottom edge of my vest slightly, waiting to be told to bare my breasts so the punishment I craved could begin. Being caned was all I could think of.

'Syra, it is time for you to make a complete commitment to me. Here,' he extended his hand towards me, 'if you take my hand I will know you are sure you wish to go forward, that there will be no more holding back.'

I touched my knee to the hard edge of the bench. I wanted to feel how unyielding it was by pressing my soft breasts against it. I wanted to know how solid the smooth surface would feel beneath me as each deliberate blow of the cane cut into my taut buttocks and I jerked beneath the impact in blinding agony. I pressed my leg harder against the edge, imagining how I would push my thighs against it, feeling its strength.

'Syra!' he said curtly, as if he knew I was lost in a dream of discipline, as if he knew he had to wake me in case I slipped so deeply into a reverie of punishment it would be impossible ever to rouse me again. 'Syra,' he repeated firmly.

'Yes...' I whispered, still pressing my leg against the bench, my mind consumed by images of the delightful pain I realised now would not come. 'Please,' I sighed, looking over at him. 'Please help me to be bad, master.'

'Yes, my pet, I will, but from now on even if I am not there you have to remember that I am still with you. I always know everything you do, in every detail. Remember, I am always watching you.'

'Please,' I repeated desperately. '*Please*...' I felt a rush of excitement as he approached abruptly, and turning me around, forced me down on my knees and pressed me against the cold bench. I felt him pulling up my skirt and exposing my buttocks, but I did not count how many times his hand swept down against them. I thought only of what other things he had in store for me, knowing that as he led me to my destiny he would always be watching.

Just when he stopped spanking me - when he judged my punishment sufficient for my misbehaviour - Eve appeared. For some reason she looked drained.

Galen told her to help me shower, and she obediently took my arm and led me up the staircase and towards the red and green doors. I did not turn to look back at our master. I heard him walking up behind us, and I did not have to check any more to make sure his eyes were on me. The pet opened the red door and then

67

stared at it with glazed eyes, as though slowly realising her mistake but incapable of doing anything to correct it.

The room I looked into was white and sterile and cold. There was a chair in the centre made entirely of brightly polished steel, and upon it Cleo sat naked, her wrists manacled to the arms and her ankles affixed to the legs with metal rings. Her mouth was forced wide open by a metal ball and she was staring straight ahead as though at a distant horizon with wide, glazed eyes. The image was burnt into my mind, the bright light and the metallic coldness of the space contrasting with the supple warmth of her naked body pinned down and unmoving, a startled look frozen on her gaping countenance.

Galen moved quickly and shut the door, obliterating the sinister picture... but it was branded into my brain forever. There was a moment of uneasy silence, a pause filled with terrible anticipation, and then Galen unleashed his anger as I watched Eve shrinking away from him, backing against the wall, into a corner, sliding slowly down to the floor until her buttocks were pressed against her heels. She looked up at him apologetically, beseechingly, as though she had been punished before for the same mistake and knew exactly what was in store - and dreaded it.

'See to Syra,' he said quietly, composing himself. 'Make her ready.'

She nodded hurriedly, obviously afraid he might reconsider, afraid he might find something else she had done wrong and punish her swiftly and cruelly without a second thought. She got up and hurried past him, avoiding the slightest proximity to his menacingly tense body. Taking my arm she opened the green door and led me into a bathroom, and I could feel her hand trembling.

I had not wished to see the pet threatened like this. I had not wanted to see her weakness and her fear, but now I knew she was not as powerful as I believed, I relished her downfall. I had thought of her as somehow better then me, more elegant, more at ease and more fearless, but now I knew if I followed Galen's instructions I could easily surpass her. When she passed me the razor and a large towel, I imagined her as a maidservant enslaved to her mistress, and considered telling her to shave me. I would watch her closely, hoping to find an error in her performance, and even if I had no reason to I would strike her with the flat of my hand before she had time to realise what was happening. After that she would flinch when I merely looked at her, and I would smile with satisfaction each time I saw the fear I so easily instilled.

After shaving carefully between my legs I took a welcome shower, cleansing myself beneath the torrent of water. Then I knelt on the floor wrapped in the towel while she combed my wet hair, pulling it out to its full length, holding it in her hand to comb through it again. Her gestures were lazy and I wanted to tell her to be more vigorous. Finally she wrapped a red velvet band around my forehead and tied it beneath my hair at the nape of my neck. Her hands trembled slightly as she caressed my cheek before leaving the room. I did not move. I knew I was waiting for something to happen and possibilities dashed through my mind... I thought about Cleo sitting in the room next door. I thought about Espartaco facing a deadly bull... but then Galen entered, followed by the pet,

68

and my mind went blank.

He stood in front of me as she bent and pulled the red band down over my eyes. It fitted across them perfectly. I could see nothing as the white-tiled world of the bathroom was suddenly replaced with blackness. I was not startled, though; it seemed natural to me, in a way it was a relief from the brightness of the clean space. I succumbed to the blindfold almost gratefully, letting my eyes close and welcoming the absence of light as a dreamer welcomes the absence of wakefulness.

My hair was lifted away from my neck, and I could tell it was Eve's hands; the touch of her fingers familiar to me now. She stroked my neck with her fingertips as she gathered my hair and held it up, teasing out the straight wet strands and bunching them together again in her hands. I felt the tension in my scalp as she pulled my hair and held it tight so not a single strand would escape and fall back down to my shoulders. I felt the skin of my temples being strained as she pulled on my roots, and experienced a slight tingling in the back of my neck as weaker, shorter hairs complained beneath the strain.

I stretched my shoulders back and absorbed the tension of the wet towel wrapped around me. It felt like a carapace enclosing me in its shell, preventing my emergence into the light and warmth of my life's darkly enchanted springtime with Galen. I twisted my shoulders and felt the fluffy material loosen. I wriggled my shoulders again, and the terrycloth fell away, catching for a moment on my bottom before descending to my supine calves and the upturned soles of my feet. I wanted to be free of it altogether. I did not want it touching my skin any more, but I did not dare move more than I already had.

I parted my knees slightly as Eve worked silently with my hair. She was plaiting it tightly, weaving it together in three thick strands that began close to the top of my head. She was braiding it into a tightly erect pillar, rising from my head like a spike. She played with the last few strands, carefully bending them into each other and stretching the plait to the very end of the longest hairs. Then she stopped and I imagined her standing back to admire her work, touching the upright braid to ensure it was perfectly vertical. Her hand slipped beneath my elbow, encouraging me to stand, and the towel fell aside as I got up off my knees. Slowly she led me forward towards the green door. I could still picture it in my mind and I knew if wanted me to go through it I would have to bend to accommodate my new hairstyle.

I straightened up again as she led me across the cool wooden floor. I pictured the space in my mind - the exposed balcony on my right, the top of the spiral staircase on my left and, in the centre of the room, the raised wooden platform. I wondered if she was leading me out onto the balcony. I wondered if Galen had decided I must be tested again before I could progress further. Or was I to be taken naked out into the street? Was I to be like the girl I had watched with the two men, held up against a dirty wall in a dimly lit alley?

I felt a light pressure on my elbow holding me back, telling me to stop. I sensed the weight of my hair tipping my head forward slightly and held my chin up to keep the braid straight. My cheeks flushed as I felt Galen's breath against them, alternately warming each one with his slow exhalations and stroking them with his essence. I did not move, and suddenly his hand was between my legs and his upturned palm was cradling my cunt. I felt shocked by the suddenness of his touch, but my surprise was immediately consumed by an overwhelming physical joy. His hand was warm and completely covered my pussy. I wanted him to lift me up on it. I wanted him to press his palm firmly against me and lift me up off the floor. But as suddenly as he had put it there, he withdrew his hand, and the wetness it left behind cooled my achingly warm flesh. I lowered my head and once again felt the braid tipping forward slightly. He held his hand against my mouth as if telling me to remain silent, and then drew it down and parted my lips with his fingertips until my mouth was gaping open. He let me stand there for a moment with my lips as far apart as they could go, and then he slid something between my teeth.

I felt the weight of a leather ball on my tongue, heavy behind my teeth. Unable to breathe through my mouth any more, I inhaled through my nostrils. The quick intake of breath nearly made me gag on the ball, and I swallowed hard as I pressed my tongue against it to keep it as far forward as possible. I felt the sides of my mouth crease inwards as a cord leading from each side of the heavy sphere was pulled tightly around my face and tied behind my neck, drawing my mouth even more firmly around the ball and pinching my cheeks painfully beneath the tension. I felt my head nodding forward and realised someone was weaving something into the top of my upright plait. I was urged forward a step, and feeling a hard edge against my toes, I realised I was standing next to the raised platform in the middle of the room.

I did not know if I was frightened or excited. Everything was so strange, so new and confusing for me. I could not make sense of everything I had experienced since arriving in Spain. I wanted to ask what was going to happen to me. Even though I knew the answer would not change anything, I still wanted to know. But, somehow, I could not even form the question in my mind much less utter it with a leather ball stuffed into my mouth. Then, as though I had asked him about my future aloud, as though he could read my mind and formed the question for me, Galen provided the answer.

'Everything you have ever desired, Syra, my pet,' he promised me. 'Everything you have ever desired.'

I have had to stop writing. I feel overwhelmed by my memories, overcome by what has built up inside me as I think about everything again. It has made my hands shake and I cannot hold the pencil still enough to write legibly. My stomach churns with anxiety when I think about how recording my experience is affecting me. When the trembling began, I put my pencil down and looked away in the hope it would stop. I thought if I ignored the way my body was shaking I would recover and soon be able to carry on, but that was a long time ago and shudders of emotion keep wracking me. He told me to keep working until he returned, but I stopped for too long and now I do not have time to catch up again. This has made me even more nervous, but I do not know what to do. If

I tell him I am unable to write my story because it is too exciting for me, he will say I have to do so anyway and start from the beginning again. I know he will say I am not sufficiently recovered and need more treatment, so I must go back to the beginning. I could not bear to start all over; I have come too far. I could not stand to go through it all again...

CHAPTER 9

I was still shaking anxiously when he arrived. He counted the pages I had written and then looked at his watch. I could tell he knew I must have stopped, that I had not done enough. I thought of shrugging, of lifting my shoulders and raising my eyebrows dismissively, but the idea made my stomach come alive with nerves. Pretending I did not care was worse than being fearful of knowing I *did* care. He asked me if there was any reason why I had written less than was expected of me. His words were a confirmation of my worst fears and, dropping my guard for a moment, I almost told him the real reason - because what I was writing about was just too exciting - but I quickly came to my senses and looked away from him. I felt him shrug in the same way I imagined myself shrugging off his question, in a way that showed it did not matter and he did not really care. I felt let down by his response. It was as though he was no longer concerned about me, as if what I was doing had ceased to be important to him. And he had not said anything about using the word *cunt* again. He made so much fuss about it before, and yet now he did not seem to care.

He sat on the step and motioned for me to bend over his knees, but even then he seemed impartial. I hung across his lap feeling the floor against the tips of my toes as I braced myself with my fingertips, waiting, expecting the worst. But even as I cried out beneath each hard smack of his hand, and kicked my legs up to try and soothe the burning pain, he did not quicken his pace or press his left hand harder into the small of my back. I climaxed, as always, when the pain was so great I knew I could no longer bear it and my body transformed it into an excruciating pleasure. But when he lifted me off his lap I felt strangely disappointed, because though I had appeared to reach my limit, in reality I was far from it.

I climbed back onto his knees, holding my sore red bottom up for more punishment, squirming against him, demonstrating my disobedience and the need for further discipline. He pushed his hand into the small of my back, and I sighed contentedly knowing it was not over yet. He gave me some more unforgiving smacks, and I gasped with shock as each blow fell. Another orgasm crested inside me as I held his ankles and jerked against his legs. The spanking continued - I felt as though it would never end - and I bit my lip and squirmed against him passionately, relishing the intense suffering, savouring the humiliation, until he suddenly shoved me off his lap and left me alone again.

71

As I stood against the edge of the raised platform I had no idea what was going to happen to me. I felt the way I had on the edge of the balcony, as though I was on the brink of something I had never experienced before, something fearful, but which I did not wish to turn away from. I was waiting to fall or be pushed into whatever lay before me.

The blindfold was drawn away from my eyes. I did not close them, but instead stared straight out into the bright room. I tried to swallow, but it was impossible with the heavy ball filling my mouth. Eve held my shoulders and turned me slightly, and I saw my vague reflection in the shiny chrome doors of the large cupboard. My hair was pulled up on top of my head into a long vertical braid, two thin cords woven into it. Its base was thick and pulled on my scalp, but it had been plaited so neatly no stray hairs were visible. The cords leading from the ball-gag were pulled tightly into the corners of my mouth before crossing my cheeks. They were pulled so taut my chin was tipped slightly downward, not so far that it touched my chest but far enough to stop me bending my head any further.

'Do you think you look beautiful?' Galen asked me as he bent down and removed the padlock from the closed doors of the hatch on the platform.

I looked at myself again, and nodded by dropping my shoulders forward, feeling the weight of the braid as it swayed slightly. I felt like an Egyptian queen bathed by her favourite servant girl and now, ritually gagged and naked, I was being presented to my lord and master for his approval. I looked earnestly at Galen, hoping he would not reject me.

He pulled the hasp and staple free, and opened the tight-fitting doors in the platform. He held them up at right angles for a moment, and then let them fall fully open. 'Step up here, Syra my pet, onto the edge, but keep your hands by your sides. Keep them there until I tell you otherwise.'

I pressed the palms of my hands firmly against the sides of my thighs, raised my knee and climbed up onto the edge of the opening. I looked down into the open hatch and saw nothing, only an abyss of blackness intersected by the bright steel running across it. I expected him to ask if I was afraid, but he did not. Then I realised it would be pointless for him to ask me anything. He knew how I would respond - or at least, how I should respond. How could I possibly be afraid if he was with me?

He stood behind me and wedged his hands beneath my armpits. His fingers touched the sides of my breasts and I felt my nipples harden as a tingling anticipation ran through me. He squeezed his fingers against my tender flesh and I sensed him encouraging me to fall into his hands. I dropped back slightly, and he accepted my weight.

'Step forward,' he instructed me quietly.

For a moment I hesitated, but that was all, only for a moment. Then I stepped forward out over the edge of the opening in the platform and into the void. He held me, my hands stiff at my sides, my gaze fixed firmly ahead and the ball-gag tightly lodged in my mouth. I did not even stretch out my toes to test the terrifying emptiness, but simply let him slowly lower me into the darkness. I felt

72

completely controlled by him. My will - what was left of it - was completely replaced by his and I did not wish it otherwise.

My toes touched something that felt like water, or silk, I was not sure which. The invisible surface presented only the slightest resistance to my initial contact, and as soon as my flesh penetrated it, I felt as though part of me vanished. It was like receiving the softest kiss as the prelude to a completely absorbing abandonment. My toes were lost in the welcoming bath, and then my calves and my knees. I felt as if they were floating away as my master lowered me into the warm black mouth of the hatch, yet I was not afraid and offered no resistance as I descended.

My breasts grazed the steel bar as he lowered me past it. It was shockingly cold, and already hard and aching, my nipples stiffened even more as the icy metal surface glided across their sensitive tips. The darkness lapped around my thighs, absorbing them, and then it touched my vulva and I swallowed hard, feeling the ball pressing against the back of my mouth. The temperature of the void exactly matched the temperature of my flesh, and as the lips of my sex made contact with it, they seemed to become one with the darkness itself. I felt as if my pussy was everything, the centre of a whole dark universe, and as though I was being slowly consumed by all the sensations latent within it. I saw the bar rising in front of my eyes and stared straight ahead as it passed my gaping mouth, the tip of my nose and my eyes.

As I descended further I felt the liquid warmth, an envelope of dark delight, spreading over my breasts and my nipples and my throat, until at last it reached my chin.

I stopped descending and hung weightless. I was floating, filled with nothing but the sensations of my invisible skin as they flowed through my mind and came together in the warm joy blooming in my submerged pussy. I was let down a little more, and I felt a tension on the end of my vertical braid as Galen released me. I floated in the darkness, knowing the cords in my plaited hair were tied to the steel bar, suspending me from my scalp in a liquid so close in temperature to that of my body it was impossible to say where my flesh began or ended. And then darkness consumed me absolutely as the doors of the hatch closed above me.

Almost at once I lost my sense of direction. In the sudden and complete blackness there was no up or down. My face was free of the water but I could not distinguish the liquid from the air. I did not know if I was spinning on the braid or whether I was held still by it. I thought about raising my arms away from my sides, but I could not quite determine where they were or how to move them. It was as though my body had disappeared.

Then suddenly images began filling my mind, pictures flashing like lightening before me in the darkness, accompanied by disembodied yet stunningly intense feelings... I smelled a myriad of fragrant scents, tasted a variety of flavours, heard musical notes and touched a world of forms and textures. I was engulfed in blackness, enveloped in a warm, all-pervading void as my mind spilled over with images and sensations like a goblet being endlessly filled and forever overflowing...

I saw Cleo, her wrists tightly manacled to the arms of the steel chair and her ankles enclosed by the heavy metal clamps. I saw her naked body sitting unnaturally upright in the chair and her startled, wide-eyed expression gazing into an imaginary distance, the shiny steel ball filling her mouth. A glimmer of perspiration glistened on the tops of her firm breasts and in her cleavage, a thin trickle like a distant sunlit river running down between the gentle mounds of her breasts and down her flat belly. I saw Eve kneeling, her buttocks pressed against her heels, between Cleo's legs. I saw her hands reach up and cover the blonde girl's delicate bosom as she pinched her nipples. I saw her long black hair draping across the top of Cleo's thighs as she burrowed her face as far between them as she could, pressing her full mouth against the soft lips of her pussy. I saw her head rising and falling as she ran her tongue over Cleo's pudenda, and I saw the bound girl's eyes widen even more as the intimate tongue found the divinely warm centre of her slit. I saw she could not move, her restraints too tight, but she tensed as each lick of Eve's tongue stoked the passionate heat rising within her. I watched her pupils dilating as the pet circled her clitoris with the probing tip of her tongue. I could see the tension in her firm young muscles as she fought to contain the rising wave of pleasure overwhelming her. Her toes strained and her calves tightened as she pulled against the unyielding clamps around her ankles. Then I saw her relax slightly as the pet moved her tongue back to the centre of her vulva, but as soon as the agile tip licked its way to the hot core of her pussy, I saw her body stiffen and then tremble as the paroxysm of an orgasm overtook her. I watched Eve increase the pressure on her nipples as she tensed beneath a long and drawn out climax. And as Cleo clenched around the steel ball stuffing her mouth, I bit down on my leather ball-gag. As her cheeks tightened so did mine, and when I saw the smoothness of her chest and throat flush pink as pleasure suffused her flesh, I felt the rush of warmth in my own invisible skin... followed by a convulsion of joy that seemed to emanate not from between my legs but from the very core of my being...

I wanted to draw my knees up against my breasts and wrap my arms around them. I wanted Eve to lick my slit as I held it open and exposed for her, displaying myself to her, the flesh of my labia pulled tight by the tension of my bent legs. I wanted to feel her tongue prising into the smooth lips, poking between them, tasting my moisture before withdrawing to tease my clitoris, forcing me to come again, not allowing me to hold back but driving me on remorselessly...

I saw Galen pulling the pet away. I was not sure whether he was pulling her away from me or from Cleo, yet I distinctly felt the loss of her probing tongue and the absence of her full lips. And then Cleo began struggling frantically against her bonds. It was as if she was panicked by Eve's loss and all the delights the other woman had filled her with. I empathised with the emptiness she was experiencing. Like her, I wanted to struggle against my bonds. I wanted to tug and thrash against the restraining manacles holding me down in the chair. I wanted to feel the pain in my wrists and ankles as I pulled wildly, with all my strength, against them. I imagined Galen loosening my bonds enough to let me wriggle free, and then I saw myself crawling around him on my hands and knees to throw myself, open-legged, in front of Eve. I lay on my back breathing through flared nostrils, my hands pressed against the insides of my thighs as I held my legs as far apart as possible. I wanted the pet to crouch between them and lap my shaved cunt, licking me as she drank my juices. I felt Galen step forward as his shadow fell across me, and I saw his open palm rise over Eve's buttocks. I waited for him to spank her as I continued forcing my legs wide open, and when his hand swooped down and I heard her gasp in pain, I raised my hips and clamped my thighs around her head. Another smack on the pet's upturned buttocks caused her to fall forward, and I felt a surge of extra pressure as her tongue pressed against my pussy. Another smack and its tip drove deep inside me. Every blow that followed, each one harder than the last, thrust her tongue deeper into my sex. Each blow that fell propelled her forward, gasping for breath as her tongue sank deeper into my juicing slit...

Eventually Galen stopped spanking her, and I threw my head back in ecstasy as I watched him walking over to Cleo. I tried to turn on my side so I could crawl after him, but again my ankles were arrested and my wrists no longer free. I could feel Cleo's heart thumping in her chest as he approached her, and my own heart pounded in empathy with her excitement. He reached down to the manacles at her ankles, and flicked them open. She stayed where she was for a moment, not moving, uncertain what he wanted, wondering what to do. But as soon as she did move he grabbed both her ankles and lifted them high, exposing her taut buttocks and her soft pink pussy lips squeezed between them. Then he closed his powerful grip around both her ankles with one hand while his other hovered before her eyes, and he waited until he saw enough terror in them to sweep it down.

My ears filled with the sharp smacking sounds as his rigid palm came down repeatedly across her buttocks. She quivered beneath every blow and I imagined her pain, but more than that, I actually felt the sharp thrills of excitement accompanying every punishing slap. Each time his hand impacted with her quivering flesh, each time it smacked against her bottom cheeks, I felt the shock of it and the hot flow of painful joy, which culminated in an explosion of terrible rapture when the side of his hand caught the edges of her unprotected sex. I do not know how many blows he delivered, how long he held her ankles high above her head or how many times she climaxed, I only know that every blow created a wave of passion which threatened to drown me in a bottomless sea of pleasure...

Cleo was gasping, panting like a dog as he took her ankles into both his hands again. He opened her legs wide, fully exposing her pussy. I felt her vulnerable nakedness and quivered at the thought of him displaying me like that. Eve stood behind him, wrapping her hands around his hips to slowly undo his belt. She pulled it away and opened his trousers, drawing the zipper down slowly. I wanted to be in her place. I wanted to push my hands into his clothes and touch his hard flesh. I wanted to hold the weight of his stiffening penis in my hands. I wanted to run my fingers along its silky length and caress every pulsating vein, every subtle, sensitive contour of his shaft, every inch of his fine skin.

Cleo gasped as she saw the heavy cock in Eve's hands. She fought with the manacles at her wrists, not in an effort to release herself, but because she longed to climb on top of him and wrap herself around him, to take his erection and ride him until he climaxed deep inside her. I felt her jaw clenching around the steel ball in her mouth and felt her desperate need to be filled. Eve urged him forward, releasing her grip on his cock only when she was sure she had fed it firmly into the wet, clinging lips of Cleo's sex. The girl's eyes widened and she tossed her head back in ecstasy as Eve wrapped her arms around him and pressed her hands against his muscular stomach. I felt Cleo's multiple orgasms blooming through her charged flesh as rapidly as gunfire, relentless shots of bliss bursting inside her, each one more intense than the last. I shuddered with every one of her climaxes and panted loudly as my master thrust into her faster and harder, lifting her off the seat while holding her up by the ankles so he could drive his erection even deeper into her slender body. I did not feel it when *he* came. It was too much for me. The heat inside me, the tightness and the strain all overcame me in one long shuddering paroxysm of joy...

A burst of brightness made me flinch and I knew the hatch above me was opening. I remained perfectly still. Even the sudden illumination was not enough to move my weightless body. I felt the braid on top of my head being released, and gradually I became aware of hands beneath my armpits again. They lifted me slowly and it was like being levitated. I did not feel the pressure of hands on me or the weight of my body beneath them. I felt as if I was floating upwards, light as a cloud. I was being returned to normality, removed from the fluid realm liberating so many passions within me, and I was stunned to realise all the vivid pleasures that had overcome me in the dark had only been fantasies, a confusion of dreams and desires released by my isolation and sensory deprivation.

Galen laid me on the floor and loosened the cords holding the ball-gag in my mouth. I felt it move against my tongue, but like the world of fantasy that had possessed me, I did not want to let it go and I hung on to it for a while, licking and biting it gently. Finally he opened my mouth with his fingers and prised it out from between my teeth. I felt a deep sense of loss and moaned pitifully.

'Syra, my pet, do not worry, you will have it back again soon.'

I lay there panting, unable to close my jaws for a few moments, hoping he would gag me again, hoping I would never have to speak again, hoping he would lower me back into the darkness and let all the erotic dreams begin afresh and last forever.

I did not want to lie on solid ground warm and satisfied. I wanted to return to the dark void that had freed so many sensations from inside me and generated so much imaginative intensity in my mind.

I rolled slowly over onto my back and stared up at the white ceiling. The braid was still there, I could feel the tension of it against my scalp, and I kept my arms at my sides. I was lying naked on my back in his presence. He could do

76

whatever he wanted to me, and the mere thought sent a fresh ripple of excitement through my blood.

I felt I could do anything, too. No pleasure was beyond my reach, no passion beyond my capacity. I wanted to test myself against everything. I felt fearless and emancipated. It was as though my life had begun anew.

I let my head loll to one side. Eve was crouching naked against the wall, her hair tangled around her face and the tip of her tongue licking her lips. I stared longingly at the dark pubic hair between her legs and at the pink flesh beneath it.

I rolled onto my other side and saw my reflection in the lower drawers of the chrome cupboard. I looked pale and drawn.

'Galen...' I whispered.

'You may take your hands away from your sides now,' he instructed, and I fully realised at last that my freedom relied entirely upon him.

CHAPTER 10

This time he seemed almost pleased with what I had written. He crossed out the word *cunt* wherever he found it, but strangely enough this did not seem like an admonishment, but rather like a routine action not threatening further punishment. I felt gratified when he nodded in agreement at something I had written, even though I did not know what it was. He stopped reading and thought about something, nodding his head slowly all the time as he pondered my statements. I thought of asking him what had caught his interest, and if he wanted to discuss it with me, but then I felt a surge of shame at even having such a thought.

When he finished reading, he told me I had done well and a wave of satisfaction washed over me, warming my skin and evoking a delectable ache between my thighs. It was the first time since I'd arrived that I felt this way. I did not know if I should tell him about it. I was not entirely sure what was expected of me and whether this feeling was a good thing, a step in the right direction, or not. I decided to say nothing, but the feeling did not go away, and as I crawled up onto his lap for my spanking, I could not get it out of my mind that although each of the smacks stinging my bottom was a punishment, it was also a reward.

Just as he left, I opened my mouth to ask him if I could carry on using the word *cunt*, but the words did not come out. My confidence had not grown *that* much. When I picked up the fresh paper to start again, I saw he had written at the top of the page, *You may use the word cunt, but you must continue always to sit up straight while you are working and when you are waiting for me to return.* I was so excited I could not wait to get started again. I took the paper to the centre of the room and sat on the floor with my back perfectly straight, and began writing.

77

I woke up and struggled to open my eyes. When my heavy lids finally lifted, I could see nothing except light. I tried to sit up, but found I could scarcely move my body it ached so much. I was surprised by the touch of a hand on my naked shoulder, and I turned my head so quickly it made me dizzy. It was Galen touching me.

'You have done well, Syra my pet. Eve, and especially Cleo, have not benefited from the treatment in quite the way you have. Though I can forgive Cleo, for she is very young and has had little preparation.'

His words made me feel proud and I stretched my stiff limbs with the languid satisfaction of a cat.

'Yes, you have done better than both of them,' he concluded. 'My floatation tank obviously suits you. Here, come and sit with me on the balcony.'

I accepted his extended hand, and completely naked, allowed him to lead me out onto the balcony.

'Does the exposure still frighten you?' he asked me, looking towards the unprotected edge.

I gazed down into the small square below us. I felt entirely different than the first time I stood there. 'No, not in the slightest,' I stated with absolute certainty.

It was that magical time just before sunset and nightfall when the world is hushed and suspended in the mysterious moment of crossing over. We sat on chairs near the edge of the balcony. I stretched my legs forward, tightening my buttocks and lifting my hips to more fully expose my shaved pussy to the world. Galen drew himself up close to me and pointed out the young woman I had seen before with the two men. She was sitting opposite the taxi driver, talking to him across a small table. She leaned forward on her elbows, and when she laughed her bright red lip-gloss glistened in the golden light of a small lamp on the table between them, accentuating the fullness of her lips and highlighting her white teeth and well defined cheekbones. Her face radiated youthful spirit and her curvaceous body exuded desirability. She sat back in her chair and tossed her long dark hair over one bare shoulder. Then she suddenly looked up at me and smiled in a casual, matter of fact way.

I shrunk back a little, embarrassed and startled.

'Do not worry, Syra, my shy little pet, she cannot see you,' Galen assured me. 'She is smiling because she is pleased.'

'What about?'

'She is pleased because tomorrow she will have plenty of money to spend. Can't you see she is agreeing to a deal, settling on a price for her favours?'

The girl stretched forward again and held up four fingers. The taxi driver nodded slowly and they shook hands. Her white teeth shone in the lamplight as she opened her mouth in a wide, becoming smile. Then they both got up and he led her into the alley where I had watched her before with the two young men. His cab was parked there. The girl leaned back against the front of the bonnet, placing her hands behind her and running her fingers across the smooth metallic surface. She ran her palms across the metal as if relishing its cool firmness. The amber glow of a streetlight just barely reached her, picking out sharply defined

78

shadows in the pleats of her short tartan skirt and highlighting her nipples as they poked stiffly against the thin white material of her blouse. The honey-coloured light shone on her smooth legs and shimmered on the bright metal buckles of her highly polished black shoes, making it look as though she was perched on two dazzling stars.

The driver placed his hands on her hips and she squirmed beneath his touch. I saw the glint of the thin metal clasp holding a narrow leather belt around the waist of her skirt. The buckle was pulled tightly up to the last hole on the belt and the remaining length, hanging down loosely, accentuated the appeal of her narrow waist. As I watched I felt a sudden shock inside me, as though I had tripped and was falling into a dream... I felt confused and for a moment forgot where I was... I could not be sure if I was sitting on the balcony or if I was standing in the alley... *I* was that young woman and the driver's hands were resting on *my* hips... I could feel against the outspread fingers of my hands the smooth metal of the vehicle's shiny bonnet... I shivered, blinked and the moment passed, but it left behind in me a shaky and profound feeling of anxiety.

I stretched my legs out further and slipped both my hands between them, resting the palms flat against the insides of my thighs so my thumbs touched either side of my soft labia. I shivered again as the grazing of my thumbnails set fresh sparks of sensation shooting through my body. I was energised by the charge of feeling as it coursed through me, tugging at my nerves. My stomach muscles tightened and I shivered again, looking desperately at Galen. I needed the reassurance of his commanding presence. I needed to know he was there, watching me and observing all my reactions because they mattered to him.

'How long was I in the tank?' I asked anxiously.

'Why do you want to know, Syra, what is worrying you?'

'How long was I in there?' I asked again breathlessly. 'Please tell me. And did I imagine those things or did I experience them?' I felt myself beginning to panic.

'Calm down, my pet. No harm has come to you. How long do you *think* you were in the tank?'

The firm sound of his voice helped clear some of the mist of my confusion. I realised I had no idea how long I had been suspended in a dark void, and I did not know what to reply. In a sense it had seemed like only minutes, and in another sense it had felt like forever. 'A few minutes?' I ventured a guess. 'Maybe more?'

'Then you have answered your own question, Syra.'

I was not reassured.

'But the things I thought I saw...' I went on hesitantly, still wanting the solid truth. 'They seemed so real. But they weren't, were they? Please tell me what's been happening to me, Galen. Were those things I saw and felt real?'

'Do you wish them to be real, Syra?'

I pursed my lips and looked down. I felt like a confused child uncertain of the world and of my place in it, because I still could not quite grasp where fantasy ended and reality began. I stared at my hands resting between my legs and could not believe I did not feel embarrassed at my nakedness and exposure. 'Yes,' I said at last, 'I do. I do wish they were real.'

'Then do not be concerned, Syra. You have nothing to be afraid of any more. Fear is not part of you now. Your fears have been exposed for the charlatans they are. Now you can be as bad as you wish. There is nothing holding you back. I promise you that now your every desire can be fulfilled. You only need to test yourself and you will have the proof you need what I am saying is true.'

That word again - *bad* - sent shivers of delight down my spine. The sound of it thrilled me intensely. It was like a parcel of bliss containing everything I had once been afraid of and everything I now desired. In some way that small, simple word held all the things I secretly wished for, every craving I ever dared have, and Galen's promise unwrapped it and laid its contents bare for me like a priceless gift. 'Can I *truly* be bad?' I asked, thrilling to my own utterance of the word. 'Truly, *truly*, bad?'

'Does it excite you to watch the young woman down there in the alley?'

'Yes, very much.'

'Does the fact that she has sold herself for money excite you?'

'Yes...'

'And does the idea of her now having to satisfy a stranger thrill you, Syra?'

My throat was dry. I could hardly speak, but after I swallowed, I said the only thing that was possible. 'Yes, it thrills me.'

'And the idea that she does not know what this stranger wants, what things he wishes to do to her, does that excite you as well, Syra?'

'More than anything,' I breathed. 'The idea of having to do something but not knowing what it is excites me more than anything.'

'Then watch.'

The driver turned the girl around and she leaned forward across the bonnet. I felt the control he had over her. He had paid for her and she had agreed to do whatever he wanted. Until the contract was satisfied, she would not be released. I could imagine how she felt now beholden to his every whim, no longer able to control what she did or what happened to her. Her only goal was to do what she was told and to strive to please him. Her only purpose was to satisfy any desires he demanded satisfied by her nubile young body. My heart pounded at the thought of being in her position, of following instructions without question, of being blindly obedient and completely submissive. It was so arousing I wanted to run down and take her place. I wanted to bend over the bonnet of the cab and wait for the first demand to be made. I wanted to experience the fear that would accompany the anticipation, and the sinking sense of hopelessness and despair tainting the dark exhilaration of being forced to satisfy a stranger's sexual demands.

The man put his hand on the girl's back and bent her fully forward across the shiny metal bonnet. Her pleated skirt lifted slightly and the pert curve of her buttocks could be seen from beneath the hem. Only the slightest crease marked the joining of her bottom cheeks to the top of her thighs, and I could see the tension in the beautifully smooth skin where it turned delicately into the

80

shadowed indentation between her legs. I sensed her willingness to bend forward in front of the man, and the easy manner with which she did so entranced me. The simple act of facing away from him and leaning forward so her unprotected bottom was thrust towards him struck me as the epitome of submissive compliance.

The driver lifted the hem of her skirt slightly, and I trembled as the white edge of her panties was revealed. I leaned forward in my chair and peered intently into the space between her thighs, but the driver let go of her skirt and it fell as if in slow motion, almost fully covering her panties again and concealing from view the white purse of her pudenda.

'Could you do that?' Galen asked me abruptly.

I was surprised by the sound of his voice. I knew I wanted to do it as I watched, as I sat safe on the balcony, but wanting was not the same as doing. 'Yes,' I said, without letting myself think about it.

'Then bend over in front of me. Get down on your knees, put your hands on the edge of the balcony, and expose your bottom, your pussy and your anus to me while you watch the scene below.'

I did not hesitate to do as he instructed. First I stood up and faced him, so he could look at me and I could enjoy the feel of his eyes on me. I hoped he would look at my breasts and see how hard my aching nipples were, and if he chose to, he could stare closely and see them lifting slightly with each throbbing beat of my heart. I wanted to see his eyes on the shaved flesh of my pussy. I wanted to watch him gazing at it intently, observing that the smoothness of my skin was broken only by goose bumps of excitement.

He indicated with a pointing finger that I should turn around and get down on my knees. My heart pounded in my chest, making it hard for me to take a deep breath as I fought to control my trembling limbs. I was filled with anticipation, bursting with a flood of expectation. It was as much as I could take. I was already very wet. How could anticipation be so fulfilling? How was it possible to be taken to your breaking point by a mere thought, without any physical contact, without the completeness of action? How could expectation itself lead me to the very brink of gratification? I turned away from his eyes and lowered myself onto my knees. I felt his gaze on my back. I could feel the heat of his stare as it penetrated every pore of my skin and made my blood boil with lust. Slowly I knelt and sat with my buttocks pressed against my upturned heels. I squared my shoulders, sat up straight and clasped my hands together behind my back. I stiffened my arms, forcing my breasts forward and tightening my stomach and thigh muscles.

'On your hands and knees,' he said sharply.

I felt a twinge of guilt that I had not obeyed his exact instructions right away, and bit my lip, feeling like a naughty girl. I had been indulging myself too much in the pleasure of submitting to him and in so doing failed to obey him, now he was disappointed in me. I unclasped my hands and planted them on the floor. Then, still facing away from him, I bent forward and knelt compliantly before him as I wrapped my fingers over the unprotected edge of the balcony. It was an

81

act of remorse; I felt it as an act of penance, the only way I could show him I was sorry for my moments of slavish pride. I lifted my buttocks as high as I could, asking him to forgive my vanity by offering him my assets. I wanted him to look at my pudenda blooming invitingly between my thighs. I wanted him to glimpse the depth of my feeling for him in the promising shadow between my bottom cheeks. I wanted him to admire the sensual dip of my back as I gripped the edge of the balcony and lowered my shoulders as far as I could. I wanted him to forgive me.

I kept my bottom high as my eyes focused again on the scene below. The young woman was still lying prone across the bonnet of the taxi, the hem of her pleated skirt still barely breaking the line of whiteness that was the edge of her panties. The driver was still standing behind her, but now he dangled a rope from his hand. He looked ominous and threatening, especially since I could not tell if she was aware of what he was holding. She was still running her hands across the shiny metal, and she was either unaware of the rope in his hand, as yet innocent of its threat, or she knew about it because it was part of their agreement and she was anticipating its bite. If she *was* anticipating it, I wondered if she was afraid of the pain it might bring her of if she was relishing the sting that would perversely feed her fulfilment. Both possibilities excited me as I eased forward slightly so my face was hanging fully over the edge of the balcony. I imagined if I went too far, if I forgot myself, that Galen would grab me by the ankles and hold me there, dangling naked and suspended on his mercy.

I did not know what to expect from the tableaux below me. I did not know what I would prefer to happen. The alternatives were confused inside me in an arousing way as I fought to find reality amongst the pictures flashing through my mind. Did I want to see him tie her down so she could not move, and would I feel the tightly pulled bonds against my own wrists and ankles if he did so? Would I wriggle in front of Galen like a captured animal desperate to free myself? I pictured the look in the girl's eyes, desperate for rescue, desperate to hold on to her courage until he decided what to do with her as already she regretted their bargain. I lifted my bottom higher as the driver swung the rope idly in his hand. The sight of its lazy, swaying motion hypnotised me. I could feel my eyes following it and could sense my mind being paralysed by the rhythmic movement. It seemed to mimic the beating of my heart and the aroused pulsing of the veins in my neck as I began breathing in time with it. I stared, entranced, at the swinging rope and the beautiful victim it threatened.

The man reached forward with the hand holding the rope. He extended his forefinger and inserted the tip beneath the hem of her skirt so the loose braids of the rope fell across her bottom. He lifted the hem slightly and exposed not just the edge of her panties but the full tight spread of them enclosing her taut young buttocks. I could see the shadowy line down the centre of the material outlining the sweet divide between her bottom cheeks, and again I revelled in the sight of the darker hollow opening up like a secret valley beneath the flimsy gusset. One of the strands of rope lay in the furrow at the centre of the gusset and its end fell between her open thighs.

I wanted him to lift her skirt higher and not pull it down again, ever. I wanted to remain suspended in that moment of time until the end of time. This was the point at which I desired all actions to pause, the moment just before something happened, the cusp of expectation, the edge of the beginning of fulfilment. I wanted to see myself watching this scene forever, never having to release the tension of my orgasm, never having to commit myself to the energy that would eventually lead to dissipation. I did not want any more. This point was the point I wanted to inhabit eternally. But it could not be. Moments like these could not last; they were too perfect.

He folded the hem of her skirt up and I watched it drape across her hips. I expected to feel disappointment, but the folded edges of the sharp pleats lying above the waistband of her panties and crumpled against her bare back sent a shiver of delight through me like the unstoppable surge of an ocean swell. He took hold of the elastic rimming her panties and pulled them down in one swift movement, exposing her abruptly, shockingly, and now there was no going back. She writhed slightly as he tugged the white cotton down to her knees, and I saw the backs of her legs tense as the material pulled into a twisted knot around them.

'Have you decided what you want to happen?' Galen asked from behind me. His question was like a flash of lightning devastating me with excitement. I was surprised and shocked and swallowed nervously as my grip on the edge of the balcony weakened dangerously. Suddenly I felt dizzy and anxious, reeling with nerves, vulnerable and frail.

'Have you decided what you want to happen?' he asked me again.

This time I felt afraid; afraid because I had not responded instantly, afraid he would abandon me as a failure once and for all. But I did not know what to say. And I did not know what he wanted to hear. But he had asked me for a decision and I knew I had to make one, fast. I opened my legs slightly, so my pussy was more fully exposed to him. I imagined his gaze on it, his dark eyes looking closely at my moist flesh, but it was not enough to distract me, I still had to give him an answer. I still had to decide what I wanted to happen down there in that dark alley. But already it was too late. I could sense my master's impatience and I could see the driver lifting the rope behind his head. He was making ready to lash it down on the girl's upturned buttocks, and within seconds it would all be over. Once the rope had bitten her skin, I would not be able to decide what I had wanted to happen. Events would have overtaken me. I would have failed. Galen would see me as inadequate and would desert me. He would find someone else to take my place and he would tell her how I was a failure like the pet and like Cleo. I would become nothing more than another failure, just another of the many young women unable to fully appreciate and take advantage of the training he made available.

The rope lifted higher as the man extended his arm. I saw the girl's bottom cheeks tighten in trepidation, and the shadow between her upturned buttocks narrowed into a thin line as she drew her lovely mounds together in fearful anticipation. She spread her hands out flat on the bonnet of the car to brace herself, extending her arms fully and tensing her shoulders. She turned her face to the side, biting down on her full bottom lip, and I saw in the amber light how she squeezed her eyes closed as tightly as she could in a vain attempt to absorb the pain she knew would be visited upon her within seconds.

Still I had not answered him. It was as though I could not fight against the distraction of the images being presented to me. It was as if even Galen's request was not enough to focus my attention away from the exquisitely promising moment below me. I felt wayward and distraught. I had lost my way and did not know in which direction to turn. But I had to speak, I had to reply, I had to tell him what I desired.

'I... I want it to happen to me...'

Had I answered correctly? Would my reply please him or had I waited too long? Had I failed?

'Watch the little drama until the end, Syra my pet, and then I will send you down into the streets and you can experience it for yourself. I will know everything you do, of course, everything that happens to you, but when you come back you will tell me everything in your own words. I will want to hear it from you and I will want to make sure what you tell me is correct. But for the moment, simply watch, my pet.'

I peered down into the shadowy alley as earnestly as I could. I watched the flailing rope and listened to the stinging blows as they fell. I saw the perspiration glistening on the girl's buttocks and saw, even in the dim light of the streetlamp, the lines of redness appearing on her smooth skin. Then I saw other men enter the alley and take their turn whipping her as two of them held her down against the bonnet. Some of them chose to spank her, and she raised her bottom higher with each smacking blow as though revelling in its force, the sound it made, and the penetrating pain it filled her with.

I watched avidly as they finally turned her over, stripped her naked and tied her firmly to the bonnet. I saw the rope lashed around her chest, binding her tightly across the breasts, and peered eagerly, trembling with shockwaves of pleasure inevitably building into an orgasm, as they drew some of the rough rope down between her legs, tugging it tightly up into the sensitive valley between her thighs before leading it back up around her trim waist.

I clutched the edge of the balcony even more tightly as I saw her legs spread wide by grasping hands, and I was seized by the clenching grip of a climax as Galen began spanking me, with each blow driving me further out over the edge of the balcony. I watched the men take the helpless young beauty in every way they desired while I, too, longed to be filled with throbbing cocks. I yearned to be penetrated by endless erections and baptised with flowing semen as countless took me repeatedly. I wanted to be tied and passed from man to man as I succumbed to every pleasure they demanded from my flesh. Then I wanted to be spread across their laps and spanked as punishment for everything I had done with them and every orgasm I had experienced. I wanted my bottom spanked like the girl in the alley, as I felt cool cum flowing over it and running like a

84

river between my thighs and over my smouldering vulva.

And when it was all over, when I was panting with fatigue, when semen was trickling from the corners of my mouth, I wanted to be freed from my bonds. I wanted to feel myself slipping off the smooth bonnet of the taxi and sinking to my knees in silent exhaustion and supplication. I wanted to experience the dizzy confusion as I knelt, used and spent, on the cobbles of the alley and attempted to wipe myself dry with the tattered cotton of my torn white panties. And then I wanted to feel again the smarting pain of a final spanking.

Suddenly he appeared in the doorway and told me to stop writing. I wanted to say I had more to do and he would not be satisfied if he read my work in such an unfinished state, but I could see he was in no mood to listen to my excuses. I put the unfinished pages down and stared at them in hopeless frustration. He said he had decided to untie me. He wanted to see how I would react to being free. It had been so long since I had not felt the bonds around my ankles I could hardly remember what it was like. He bent down and slowly untied the thin rope. I looked at the back of his neck as he worked to loosen the tight knot. It was as though he was my servant, as though he was tending to my needs, almost as if he was *my* captive. I imagined he was worshipping at my feet, holding them in adoration, letting them rest in his upturned palms, caressing their soles and running his thumbs up around my ankles. I thought of him prising his fingers between my toes, gently easing them apart, and pressing his fingertips into the soft indentations between them. I sat up as straight as I could and my head drooped back. I moaned as the tension around my ankles eased, and I let my knees sag apart as the rope finally fell away.

CHAPTER 11

I spent the time he was away with my thighs apart. I kept the soles of my feet together and let my knees sink sideways until they touched the floor. I did it so slowly I could barely see my legs moving, and the tension caused the muscles in the insides of my thighs to form broad hollows at their tops. I followed the sight of them upwards and stared at the soft, fleshy mound resting there. My pubic hair had grown back a little, but still did not cover any part of the pink shadowy rift of my pussy. I pressed my hands flat on the floor behind me and moved my feet apart, stretching my legs wide and flexing my toes. I continued sitting up straight, of course, but I was determined not to let my ankles touch each other, and when I felt like sleeping, I pulled myself up against the wall so even while I slept my legs would be wide apart and my pussy fully exposed.

I think he must believe I am getting better. His attitude has changed. He is not so critical about my work any more, and although the beatings continue, untying my ankles felt almost like letting me go. I wonder if that will ever happen. I have been resigned to the way things are for so long I hardly think of being released. I do not even know where I am and I cannot remember coming or being brought here. I have begun to wonder how long I have been a captive, but I cannot work it out.

Each period of darkness slips into the next and only the interludes of work separate them, so I do not know how long they last. I wondered how long it had taken my pubic hair to grow back, but I gave up trying to work it out. I must keep on with my story. It is the only way of finding out what has happened to me, and perhaps it is the only way of finding out what is to become of me.

With my head hanging over the edge of the balcony, I flicked my tongue out and ran the tip around my dry lips. I was not aware of focusing on anything. I was simply staring, peering into the mixture of light and dark below me. Slowly my eyes came back into focus, and when I looked into the alley the taxi had gone and there was no one there. I blinked in case I was mistaken, but a nervous emptiness in the pit of my stomach told me the scene had changed. The players had vanished and with them the images inflaming my imagination. I felt like moaning in despair, like striking my fist against the balcony in frustration, but instead I licked my lips again and rocked back and forth on my aching hands and knees.

I felt a hand stroking my bottom, moulding it into its palm, reawakening my senses, bringing me back into the world. I lifted my buttocks to let the hand know I was enjoying its touch; that I was responding to it. The hand slipped between my thighs and lightly fingered the lips of my pussy, which was still aching with desire.

'After you have slept a while,' Galen said quietly, 'you will go in the taxi and do whatever you are told to do by the driver and anyone else. Face your fears and bring out your wickedness. Do you understand what I want from you?'

I nodded, but it was a vague nod and he was not content with it. He wanted to hear me say the words.

'Do you understand, Syra?' he demanded gently but firmly. 'Speak to me and tell me you understand.'

'Yes, I understand,' I whispered. 'I must do whatever I am told by whomever tells me. I must face my fears and bring out my wickedness.'

'Remember, how bad you can truly be will be tested by the unknown. Do not expect anything to be either as it appears or as you have already seen. Facing your fears will make you confront things you did not even know you feared. It is the only way you can hope to be set free into a world of complete and fulfilling pleasure.'

His words chilled me. There was something menacing about them, as if he was pronouncing a sentence on me I might not survive. I shivered and tensed my arms in an effort to lift myself up. His hand moved caressingly up my back to between my shoulder blades. He pressed down and I lowered myself again, crouching like an obedient puppy, my face hanging over the edge of the balcony, waiting until he decided to release me. He kept me there with only the gentlest pressure. I needed nothing more. In fact, I did not even need his touch or his commands. His will was strong enough to hold me and I was helplessly subject to it. But it was not merely the pleasure of humiliation driving me on. Subjecting myself to his will ultimately would lead me to my freedom, to the release of my unconfined wickedness. The chill I had felt faded, warmed by a hot wave of expectancy surging through my body as I wondered what lay in store for me.

At last he let me go, but I did not move until he held my arm and encouraged me to get up. I stood in front of him, but I was a different person than the last time I faced him this way. I had changed since I knelt before him and clung to the unprotected edge of the balcony while he smacked my bottom and I trembled in the throes of a violent orgasm watching the brutally sensual scene down in the alley. Now all I wanted was to go out into the world and test the limits of my sexuality, of my wickedness, of my self.

'Go and sleep,' my master urged, 'and then, when you awake, dress like the girl you were watching in the alley and go down and wait at the front door. The driver will pick you up there.'

I went obediently through the green doorway, spread myself on the small bed in the corner of the shower room and went to sleep.

When I awoke, what felt like only a short time later, my limbs were uncomfortably stiff. I got up and stood in the shower letting the heavy stream flow down over me like a waterfall, relaxing my stiff muscles as I languidly washed. The cold dousing refreshed me, and afterwards I did not dry myself, but let the water drip from me as I poked amongst the clothes in the wardrobe. I found a short blue pleated skirt very much like the girl's from the alley, and a white blouse. There were also some white cotton panties, smooth and delicate, that hugged my bottom when I pulled them on. I stroked my hand across them, feeling their softness encasing my buttocks, and then I slipped a finger beneath the elasticised edge, testing their tension as they pulled snugly against my flesh. I smoothed the gusset against my labia and relished the way it moulded to the soft lips.

I then combed my hair back while it was still wet and put on the rest of the clothes. I found some light-blue high-heeled sandals, and then I stepped out onto the redwood floor of the upper level and looked around for Galen. He was not around, so I walked down the spiral staircase and across the ground floor terrace to the front door.

It was a lovely night and the air outside was warm and fragrant with the scent of citrus and camellias. The taxi pulled up at once. The driver leered at me through the window before leaning back and opening the rear door from the inside. '*Senorita?*' he said, with mock solicitude as he pushed the door open.

I slipped into the back, feeling different to when I was last in the vehicle; more confident, more assured and more determined.

He drove off and I spread my bare arms across the back of the seat. The warm air blowing in through the window fanned coolness beneath my armpits, and the delicate perspiration dewing my skin was blown dry by the buffeting breeze. I felt as though I was the principle player in a drama, as though I was acting something out, as though Galen had written a story for me and I was simply following the script. First I would dress like the girl I had watched in the alley, and then the cab would pull up at the door and drive me to another alley just like it. There I would lean against the bonnet of the car and be tied and thrashed and fucked in every imaginable way by men waiting to take their turn with me. My stomach churned with excitement. I hoped I could do it. I knew this was my ultimate test. I knew this was what Galen had planned for me. I knew I must not fail him, because failing him would also mean failing myself, and I could not bear that.

We drove through tree lined streets in which large houses were set back from the road behind high stone walls. The smell of citrus was everywhere and I tilted my head back and inhaled it deeply. Its freshness filled my senses and I felt energised, as if the tangy scent transported me back to when I was an innocent girl with nothing to fear or to worry about. The cab came to a stop and I heard the laughter and shouting of teenage girls. Over the low wall of a convent school, lissom female students were taking advantage of the cool night air and playing netball under the supervision of two nuns, the fading light, and that coming from a few windows overlooking the yard, just enough for them to play in for a little while yet.

The driver opened my door and pointed to the wall. I widened my eyes, not knowing what he meant at first, and then I realised he wanted me to bend over it. I saw one of the girls lazily toss the ball into the net and a loud cry of joy went up as the victorious team embraced each other, giggling happily. The nuns blew their whistles and shepherded them back to the centre of the yard as I emerged from the cab and stood against the wall. The rounded top rose to the middle of my thighs and the stone felt warm as I pressed against it.

'*Inclinate*,' the driver told me sternly. 'Here.'

Another goal, more shouts and the scoring team ran elatedly around the yard hugging each other. The nuns blew their whistles, but this time their charges were too excited to come to order immediately.

'*Inclinate!*' the driver snapped.

With relief I realised we could not be seen in the shadows, so I bent forward over the wall and felt my lower tummy curve over the rounded stone ledge. I stretched my hands down to the ground and touched it with my fingertips. The girls were shouting excitedly and the whistles were blowing as the driver lifted the hem of my blue pleated skirt. I felt the exposure as he revealed my white panties, and I imagined him glaring lustfully at the fine material pulled tightly across my smooth buttocks. He held the hem of my skirt up and I knew he was looking at me closely, staring at the shadowy crease in the centre of my panties and gazing down at the gently bulging flesh of my pudenda squeezed firmly into the tight cotton. He took the hem of my skirt and laid it down across the small of my back, exposing the top edge of my panties along with the thin strip of flesh between them and the waistband of my skirt. I braced myself on the ground with my fingertips and strained to look up so I could watch the nuns and their

88

wayward students. The sisters were still struggling to bring them to order and one of them was tussling with a knot of excited girls in an attempt to pull them apart.

I felt the driver's fingers slip beneath the waist of my panties, lifting it away from my skin and peeling them down over my buttocks. He used both hands to expose my bottom, little by little. As he pulled the soft cotton away from my vulva, I felt the warm juices of my pussy making the material stick to my labial lips, and when it came free, I relished the cool caress of the evening air against my nakedness. He drew the panties down my thighs, twisted the material and wedged it just above my knees before letting it go. My nipples hardened against my blouse and I swallowed hard as my mouth went dry with anticipation.

I saw one of the nuns pulling two of the girls apart; they were fighting each other for the ball. She looped her arm around the waist of one of the girl's and spun her around, then grabbed the rebellious student's pink panties and tugged them down just far enough to expose firm young buttocks. I licked my lips and gasped as the first smack landed on my waiting bottom. I felt every part of the driver's open hand as it made contact with my flesh, each finger a burning, smarting strip stinging me, and I clenched my cheeks to absorb the pain. Then, before I had time to recover, he spanked me again even more viciously. I sagged over the wall as I watched the nun reprimanding the two disobedient girls. As the driver spanked me I watched the sister raise her own hand and bring it down on the bare bottom of her squirming, wilful pupil. The driver kept spanking me and the nun was nearly as relentless with her charge. My fingertips clawed at the ground in an effort to brace myself against the ecstasy flowing through my body and culminating between my thighs in a breathtaking climax.

Then I heard him opening his trousers, sensed him pulling out his erection, and an instant later a flood of semen coated my burning buttocks, cooling them wickedly. With the sight of the nun holding the girl in the crook of her arm and spanking her fixed in my mind, I stiffened and closed my eyes as I suffered another explosive convulsion of pleasure between my thighs.

Eventually I wearily turned, sank to my knees and sucked the driver's diminishing cock until it ceased pulsing between my lips, and I had swallowed the last seepings of his ejaculation.

About an hour later the cab stopped at the junction of two busy roads. The driver turned his head to one side and spoke without looking at me. '*Bajate*,' he commanded.

I did not understand him. I thought perhaps he was picking someone else up or was complaining about being stuck in the traffic.

'*Bajate!*' he shouted, leaning over the front seat and opening the back door for me. 'Here!'

I felt confused, but I got out and stood on the pavement.

He smiled mockingly and drove off. People jostled me and my ears were filled with the din of traffic. I felt abandoned and my stomach sank as my heart pounded. Galen had deceived me. He had given up on me, tossed me aside and rejected me because I could not meet his expectations. I looked around, not knowing what to do.

A hand fell heavily on my shoulder. 'Ah, the little experiment,' Mora declared, in his thick Spanish accent. 'So, Galen delivered you as he promised.'

My heart started beating harder and faster, this time not with the anxiety of disappointment but with relief and anticipation of fulfilment. Galen was not rejecting me. This was part of his plan. This was part of his test for me. This was how he was making me face my fears, the way he was teaching me how to let myself go completely. I hung my head and waited for Mora to tell me what to do, knowing whatever it was it would be part of Galen's plan. I had no reason to feel alone, for my master had assured me he would know everything that happened to me even before I told him about it. A shiver of excitement travelled up my spine as I thought of standing naked in front of Galen and telling him all I had done, knowing that when I finished he would bend me over his lap and spank me no matter what.

'Follow me,' Mora commanded as he turned and walked quickly along the crowded pavement swinging a closed umbrella in one hand.

I walked behind him with my head lowered, watching his footsteps and following directly in his path. I imagined I had a rope around my neck and he was leading me to a market to sell me. I was just his chattel, his possession - his slave. I displeased him somehow so he was getting rid of me. He was going to pass me on to someone else, perhaps someone more cruel. My new master would be heartless and brutal. He would begrudge having paid for me, so he would keep me on starvation rations and give me no clothes to wear. My only value would be as an object to sell to strangers for sex. But even that did not raise enough money to please him so he would beat me every night and lock me in a small cupboard. He would leave me there under orders not to move or speak, and he would only let me out to gratify the increasing demands of the men he found to use me...

Mora stopped at the entrance to a shop. The window was dimly lit, but I could make out a sparse display of several items of women's underclothing - a pair of pale green panties, a thinly cut suspender belt in what appeared to be black satin, and a bright blue basque made from velvet with vertical ribs and elegant hand-worked suspenders. The double doors leading into the shop were large and constructed from heavy smoked glass, with chrome handles and chromium frames. Mora looked into the window, slowly studying the items displayed there. I waited behind him and felt perspiration breaking out on the back of my neck.

Someone opened an umbrella as they passed by on the pavement, and its shadow fell over me like a threatening spectre. I looked up and saw that no stars were visible through the dense cloud cover. The air was thick and moist and it was difficult to take a deep breath. There was an electric expectancy in the atmosphere, as though the world was about to end in a sudden cataclysm. I felt a drop of rain land on my shoulder. It was heavy and warm, and was followed by another drop, and then another landing on my forehead like a baptismal

90

blessing. I held my breath... and the night exploded in a violent deluge. The downpour stunned me even as it seemed to awaken me, filling me with a charge of new energy, and the warm, pounding water flowed over my skin like a divinely drenching orgasm.

Mora pushed me into the shop doorway and pressed up against me. He wormed his hand between my legs and squeezed my pussy. He lifted me up on his palm, driving two fingers between my sex lips, straining the gusset of my panties and threatening to tear them. 'I will buy you something,' he said roughly, and shoving the door open with his shoulder, pulled me into the shop.

He approached a woman sitting at a desk. Although seated, I could tell she was tall, and her dark hair was pulled into a tight bun at the nape of her neck. She was wearing a black suit with a white blouse beneath it. She looked up at him and he spoke to her in Spanish. She glanced at me almost disapprovingly, and then went and produced a box from a drawer in a large wooden cupboard. The box was filled with expensive panties. Mora poked about amongst them, selected a pair of white silk with finely embroidered edges, and handed them to the woman, who was standing beside him.

'Si, senor,' she said with a dower expression. She folded the panties carefully and wrapped them in white tissue paper before placing them in a small shiny bag.

Mora turned and stared at me. He spoke to the woman again as he held my eyes, and again she glanced at me with apparent disdain. I felt embarrassed by her unsettling animosity, and out of place in the rich surroundings. 'Go to the changing room and take off the panties you are wearing,' he commanded. 'Put them in the waste bin and then come back here. The assistant will watch you, and if you do not obey correctly, she will punish you. And if she does, I do not want to hear your complaints.'

He said nothing more and I did as I was told, following the stern woman to the changing room. She stood in the doorway, staring at me as I pulled down my panties. They were wet and stuck deliciously to my labia as I peeled them off. Observing them, she tossed her head back and tutted haughtily. I looked around for the bin, trying all the time to avoid her penetrating gaze. There was a small wicker basket near the door. I moved closer and tossed the panties in, but they landed over the side and did not fall to the bottom. I saw her derisive scowl reflected in the mirror as she shook her head, knew I had done wrong, and lowered my eyes anxiously.

She took a leather-covered clothes brush from a drawer, drew up a chair and sat down upon it. She rubbed the back of the brush against her black skirt, testing its smoothness and friction. Still I did not move, watching her from lowered eyes as she lifted herself slightly off the chair and pulled up the hem of her skirt, until I caught a glimpse of her black panties and suspender belt. The whiteness of her thighs above the tops of her stockings thrilled me, and I shivered. She relaxed back on the chair and pressed her knees together. The shiny blackness of her panties was squeezed between her thighs and I imagined the fleshy lips of her pussy pressed closely against the material. She looked at

91

me and shook her head again before nodding towards the box with the fresh panties. She watched me intently as I unwrapped them from the tissue paper with trembling hands, and slipped them on. Then she sternly nodded again, this time down towards her lap.

I could hardly believe what I was doing, submitting to a stranger like this for such a trivial reason, allowing myself to be subjected to her will so easily, knowing she was going to punish me until she was satisfied I had been sufficiently reproved. But I went to her, and bending my knees, folded myself across her lap. I felt a suspender clip digging into my hip. My bottom was still covered by my skirt, but I felt exposed anyway, completely subject to her will, expectant and craving. She lifted the hem of my damp skirt and folded it across the small of my back. I shivered again with apprehension as she rubbed the back of the brush lightly against my buttocks.

I turned my head slightly and looked at the reflection of us in the changing room mirror. She sat with her back straight, her black suit immaculate, and I was draped like a sacrifice across her knees, my skirt across my back and my bottom curved upwards as she raised the leather-backed brush high into the air above me...

When she brought it down I cried out in surprise and pain, and when she smacked me viciously with the hard wooden surface again I screamed in agony and thrust a hand back to protect myself. But she merely snatched my wrist contemptuously and twisted my arm up against my back. The brush came down a third time and I wailed again so loudly my breath caught. The brush swooped down again and again, the stinging blows reddening my skin through my panties and making me squirm and howl like a trapped animal. But I did not take my eyes from the enticing image in the mirror, watching her austere expression and the brush in her hand whilst listening to my cries as though they were coming from someone else. I saw the curve of my flaming bottom emerging from the panties as they hiked up slightly, and watched my legs kicking like those of a petulant child.

Then suddenly, like an unheralded flash of lightning on a clear summer day, I shrieked and stiffened as a fiery orgasm scorched every cell in my tormented body. She kept on beating me, but I felt no more pain. My anguish was consumed by the ecstasy crashing through me, the erotic image in the glass fading as I was completely and utterly overcome.

The woman eased me off her lap and I slumped, barely conscious, to the floor. I could hardly rouse myself, but as she rose elegantly and strutted back out into the main shop area, I struggled to my feet, pulled down my skirt and followed her. She stood behind her desk and stared at me as I blushed with embarrassment.

Mora was relaxing in a velvet-covered chair, but he stood abruptly when he saw me and walked out of the shop.

As I followed in his wake, feeling weary and somewhat bedraggled, I did not actually look for Galen, but I knew that even if he was not watching me he was somehow aware of what was happening to me. Somehow he would be assessing, checking on my performance.

Outside it was still raining hard. I walked behind Mora while he strode ahead of me holding the umbrella over his head to protect himself from the storm. I was soon soaked to the skin and glad it was a warm night. Nevertheless, my blouse felt cold clinging to my naked breasts and was effectively transparent. My skirt was drenched and water dripped from the pleated ends, running down my legs in meandering rivulets. We walked away from the busy bar-lined streets into a deserted residential area, and he finally stopped before a large wooden door. Without even looking back at me to make sure I was still there, he told me to wait outside. Then he entered the house and locked the door behind him, leaving me out in the rain.

As usual I did not know what was going on. I stood out in the rain feeling at first lost, and then increasingly frightened. Trying to hold despair at bay, not knowing what else to do, I crouched on the doorstep and wrapped my arms around myself in a vain attempt to shelter my body from the rain. I stayed there all night, closing my eyes as much from shame as exhaustion. I dozed off occasionally, but every sound and every passing car put me on the alert and I sat up, my heart hammering in my chest, until the threat, as well as the promise, had passed.

The next morning, just as it was getting light, Mora finally opened the heavy door again. I felt wretched as he nodded his approval that I was still there and waved me inside. I had to squeeze past him, and he reached out and tugged my hair, holding me back for a moment to stare down into my eyes before allowing me through.

Inside the house was dark and cold. I shuddered and hugged myself to try and stop shivering. My blouse was still wet and moulded to my curves. Light glowed dimly through a pair of narrow glazed doors on the far side of the room, opening onto what appeared to be an enclosed terrace. He walked towards the doors and I followed him obediently. The sound of my footsteps on the dark-grey flagstones echoed against the high vaulted ceiling, and I shivered violently as my damp clothes chilled me to the core.

When we stepped out into the courtyard I was bathed in light, and immediately the warmth of the rising sun made me feel better. I relaxed my arms and looked up, welcoming the radiant heat. Buildings rose around the terrace, ornate balconies embellished with florid rococo ironwork clinging to their sides.

'Would the little experiment like some breakfast?' Mora asked me, but did not wait for a reply. 'Perhaps the little experiment is cold after her night out in the street? Could you not find anyone to keep you warm? I hope Galen will not be disappointed with you.' He pulled out a chair for me and I sat at a small iron table laid out with breakfast. He turned back towards the French doors, shouting for someone, and a female figure appeared carrying a tray. As she emerged I recognised her at once. It was Cleo. She looked worn out; the smooth skin of her face was dirty and her eyes were ringed with dark circles. Her sun-bleached blonde hair was tangled and greasy and stuck to her forehead and cheeks. She was barefoot and wore only a short white cotton shift barely covering her bottom. Her knees were red, and as she came closer and set the tray down on the table, I saw her fingernails were broken. I looked at her compassionately, hoping to exchange a sympathetic glance with her, as we were both Galen's experiments, but she kept her head down and did not catch my eye.

'Another little experiment,' Mora sighed, 'but not a very successful one, I think. Poor Galen has so many failures.' He ordered Cleo to leave and she shuffled away with her arms hanging limp at her sides. I could not believe how changed she was. It seemed only yesterday that Juan Carlos had brought her to Galen at the bullring. She was so lively and full of vitality then... it made me nervous to realise I could not be sure how long ago it had been. I felt a rush of confusion, and for a second I did not know where I was or even *who* I was. I thought of the things that had happened to me lately and realised I did not know if days or weeks had passed since I arrived in Spain. My sleeping patterns were erratic, and I could not remember eating any square meals. I could recall only that olive oil soaked bread, and I dug into the breakfast before me like a starved cat. There were eggs and sausages, a deliciously strong coffee made with milk, and freshly baked bread.

'Will you be another failed experiment, I wonder?' Mora mused, gazing at me as he patted his mouth delicately with a serviette. 'Will you be the next failure?' he said more bluntly. 'Or will the brave and courageous Espartaco beat you to it?' He took a final sip of coffee before patting his mouth with the serviette again and adding, 'But who cares anyway?'

He called for Cleo again and she returned despondently. He told her to clear the table and she obeyed him at once, carefully placing everything on the tray. Then he made her bend down and pick up some crumbs that had fallen to the floor. Obediently she got down on her reddened knees and brushed them up with a cloth. He watched her carefully, and then told her the floor needed washing. She looked up at him waiting for further instructions, and he ordered her to fetch a bowl and a cloth.

She took the tray away, and returned carrying a blue plastic bowl filled with water in one hand and a white cloth in the other. 'Where shall I start, sir?' she asked quietly, her voice now reflecting uncertainty rather than confidence. Her vigour and energy seemed to have disappeared completely, replaced by absolute humility and an acceptance to serve and please.

'Here,' he said, indicating the place with his foot. 'Start here. Put your bowl and cloth down near where you must begin and then get down on your hands and knees.'

She did as he instructed, sinking to her hands and knees, and then waiting for his next command. I stared at her supple body, her slender legs and tight calves, the dip in her back describing a taut curve between her tight buttocks and shoulder blades. She hung her head and her tangled hair fell forward around her face, hiding it from view.

I felt a sudden pang of envy. Why was Cleo being tested and not me? Was Galen favouring her? Was she more convincing than me about her need to express herself and overcome her fears? Had I failed already? Had there ever been a chance of success? Or was this all part of the test being set for me? I did not know, I could not work it out, but I still had faith in Galen. He had told me to do whatever I was asked. He had told me he would always be watching. He would know everything that happened to me. Mora said Cleo had failed. Perhaps this was her punishment. But her punishment - if that's what it was - thrilled me like a reward, so it could not be a punishment and she could not have failed. Her position was too delectable. How could she have failed when the penalty for her failure was so delightful?

Mora lifted the hem of her shift and exposed her smooth buttocks. Her legs were close together and I could see only a thin dark shadow drawn between the firm curves of her bottom cheeks.

He pulled her shift across her back until her buttocks and waist were completely exposed, and she remained motionless while he walked over to a cupboard and pulled out a length of course braided rope. He returned and held it above her back, swinging it and letting the ends glance lightly against her skin, tantalising her, making her feel the restraint he had imposed on her merely with words.

He halved the rope and held the looped middle beneath her waist. He wound two strands around her, pulled them through the loop and up between her legs. He drew them between the lips of her labia and then up between her buttocks, pulling them tight before tying them back into the waistband he had created.

Then he straightened up and led out the two spare ends from the knot he had made between the waistband and the twin braids rising up between her buttocks. She did not move as he did all this, but simply crouched there and let him bind her - a passive victim unable and unwilling to resist any of his desires.

I felt my heart rate quicken as he pulled at the rope to check its tightness. He touched the inside of one thigh, and she opened them slightly. He pulled the rope again, and I saw her wince with suppressed discomfort as the twin braids between her legs twisted into her short pubic hair and pinched the soft creases of her labia.

When satisfied he stepped back, holding the two rope ends together in one hand. The strands running up between her legs merged in the soft, fleshy notch of her cunt. They parted the folds of flesh enough to become buried in them, and at the centre of her entrance the ropes were pulled in so tightly they were not visible at all.

Mora put pressure on the ropes in his hand, pulling them slightly, and she shuffled backwards on her knees. Then he walked past her a few steps and led her forward. He flicked the ropes gently, giving them only the slightest tug, and she picked up the cloth and dipped it into the bucket of water. She wiped the floor with it, and he held her there while she worked. When he was satisfied and wanted her to move forward to a fresh spot, he flicked the ropes again and she responded instantly.

I only realised I was staring at the scene with my mouth open when I glanced up at one of the balconies and saw a man looking down at us. As soon as I closed my mouth, I felt the dryness of my lips and licked them.

Mora was leading Cleo forward as she mopped the floor, facing away from the spectator on the balcony. I stared at the man watching us, and suddenly knew what I wanted to do. I wanted to lift my skirt and show him my new lace panties. I wanted to spread my legs and show him how quickly I could bring myself to a climax by rubbing my clitoris through the fine white fabric.

Then I wanted to peel the panties away from my wet sex and let him see my blooming flesh and the way I touched it.

I wanted to show him the way I inserted two fingers between the moist petals of my labia and I wanted him to see the glistening of my fingertips as they came into contact with my warm wetness. I wanted him to see by the way I stretched my legs out straight that I had teased myself enough, and as I lifted my hips high, I wanted him to sense the draining pull of energy deep in the centre of my body heralding the onslaught of an orgasm. I wanted him to watch as I pressed my fingertips around the base of my throbbing clit and sank down on the chair, trembling in ecstasy.

That was what I wanted when I caught him staring at me, but when I looked away and saw Cleo working to clean the floor, I knew I also wanted to be in her position. I wanted to submit to a master who would control me like that, who would bind me in the same way, tightly and firmly, and with the merest flick of his hand command me to move either forward or back. I wanted a master who, with only the merest suggestion of movement, could hold and control me, body and soul.

I licked my dry lips again, my breath becoming swifter and shallower as I imagined myself on my knees, tied tightly with rope and made to work until my master decided I was finished with my chores. I felt the harshness of the stone tiles against my knees and smelled the dank wetness as the water from my cloth penetrated them. I felt the splash of water on my hand as I dipped the cloth into the bucket and experienced the strain on my arm as balancing on one hand I struggled to keep myself from falling over. I heard the smack of his palm on my buttocks if I did not do my job correctly, and sensed the heat from his hand as he brought it down time after time on my exposed and reddening cheeks.

I shifted restlessly on the chair, moving towards the edge of the seat, feeling myself losing control. Should I get on my hands and knees and invite Mora to tie me up and use me to serve him? Should I show the man on the balcony how excited I was? Or should I just wait until I was told what to do? I knew this was all part of Galen's test for me, but I did not know how to react. I wanted to release my wickedness so much I was not afraid of anything any more. I wanted to take myself to the limit...

Suddenly, a feeling of emancipation came over me like a sudden blast of fragrant air, like a heavenly zephyr blown by a beautiful god. It was a wind of rebirth, of realisation, and it seemed to lift me up off the chair as I became lighter than a feather. I glanced at Mora. He was still not looking my way, so I stretched back, lifted my skirt and fed three fingers deep into my pussy, not gently caressing it, not teasing its soft edges or urging my clitoris to expose itself. I simply sought out my depths with a burst of animal lust, ravaging myself, opening myself wide, and revealing the dark pink interior of my cunt to the man watching from the balcony.

Mora did not see, but I could not believe he did not hear me coming. Afterwards I pulled my skirt down as far over my thighs as possible and placed my clasped hands on my knees in a prim schoolgirl pose. I turned slightly away from the man on the balcony and stared fixedly at Cleo. I watched her until she finished her work and as Mora untied the ropes and told her to get up and go.

She did not look at him. She did not nod or acknowledge him in any way. She simply obeyed him. I sat still and waited. I would not question anything he ordered me to do.

He left me there for the rest of the day, appearing only briefly to tell me I had permission to relieve myself. Then I returned to the courtyard and continued waiting for him, sitting silently, until he finally came back in the early evening, looking very pleased with himself.

'Well now, little experiment, where shall I put you for the night? Should I make you wait outside again? Should I leave you to the mercy of the streets? Or should I keep you inside, safe and secure?'

After sitting for so many hours my senses were dazed, but now I felt a surge of expectation awaken them like a dazzling light filling my mind and hiding all thoughts from me. I wanted him to put me outside the door again. I wanted to sit on the threshold as strangers walked by and leered at me. I wanted to offer myself to them, to as many as wanted me in as many ways as they wished to take me. I wanted to bend over, my bottom exposed to every passer-by who felt like spanking me until my cheeks were a flaming red and tears were streaming down my face from the pain...

'Whatever you wish,' I heard myself say, and the words thrilled me. I was committing myself just as Galen had said I should.

Mora took my hand and led me back into the gloomy house. I was sure he was taking me to the front door, and shivered with excitement at the thought of being outside again all night. But he stopped by a large piece of furniture in the entrance hall. I could hardly make it out in the shadows, but as my eyes adjusted, I saw it was a large, heavily constructed cupboard with two mirrored doors, a large drawer near the base, and around the edges it was extravagantly decorated with an intertwining profusion of carefully sculpted leaves and flowers.

'No, I think I will keep you inside for tonight,' he said thoughtfully, and opened the double doors of the cupboard. I smelled the tangy scent of cedar and the heavy aroma of mahogany as the doors pulled out and displaced the cool air.

The inside of the wardrobe was divided into a wide shelf at the top, a deep shelf split vertically into three partitions in the middle, and a further wide shelf below them.

'You will stay in here for the night,' he informed me. 'Undress and get into the middle section of the centre shelf. It will be cramped, but you will fit. You will stay there until I release you in the morning. While you are in there you must

97

remain still and you must not shout to be released or make any noise whatsoever. Is that clear, little experiment?'

'Yes,' I said, already unbuttoning my blouse. I dropped it on the floor, and then pulled the thin belt at the front of my skirt undone. I undid the top button and the zip at the side and it fell around my ankles. I stood there for a moment in case he wanted to look at me, but he showed no interest, so I stepped forward and climbed into the centre section of the divided wardrobe wearing only my lace panties. I had to turn sideways to fit, and I could only wedge myself into the space with my knees pulled up to my chin and my arms wrapped tightly around my legs. I had to bend acutely and wedge my forehead against my knees to get it beneath the shelf above me, and I felt the pressure of it against my neck.

I waited for him to close the doors, my pulse accelerating and my hands perspiring as I clasped them around my shins. Then the doors closed with a heavy thump, echoed by my heart, and I was enclosed in pitch darkness until he decided to release me.

The door was suddenly flung open and I gasped with fright. I was so lost in my story I thought it was Mora returning to let me out of the wardrobe.

My heart was thumping. I felt confused and for a moment I didn't know where I was. It was as though I had lost contact with myself, as if I was no longer in a position to collect my own thoughts.

I lifted my work and held it out to him, hoping I was doing the right thing, hoping I had not annoyed him by being caught unawares. He stood on the threshold for a few seconds, and then turned and left as abruptly as he had come, slamming the door behind him. I knew he would be back so I bent over my work again and awaited his return.

CHAPTER 12

I was relieved when at last he did return, made me stand up and bend over, and rubbed his hand a few times across my bottom before spanking me. He has left me feeling very sore - the punishment was hard - but the stinging redness of my buttocks only makes me want to get on with my work and submit it to him again for his approval. It seems ridiculous to feel like this. I should feel afraid and hopeless, I know I should, but I do not. Reminding myself again of being in the wardrobe has made my captivity here even more of a dark joy.

I can see he is puzzled by my behaviour. Perhaps he thinks there is no cure and I can never be saved from the malady of myself. Or perhaps he is impatient. Perhaps I have not done as well as he hoped I would and he cannot be bothered to bring about a proper cure. All I know for certain is that I have more to write and his impatience tells me I must get on with it.

98

Nothing I had ever experienced before prepared me for my first night in the cupboard. I was so keen to be shut in, so quick to strip off my clothes and get inside, to crouch in the small space clutching my legs in my arms with my head bent against my knees touching the shelf above me, but I did not know then why I felt that way. I did not know whether it was because Mora had told me to do it - because I knew whatever he told me was part of Galen's plan - or whether there was some other reason, some different level of desire driving me to bury myself in the darkness and stay there silently until released.

It was so quiet when he closed the doors I could only hear my heart beating and the sound of my short, gasping breaths. I kept my eyes closed for a long time, concerned only with the vivid images in my mind... I saw Cleo cleaning the floor with the rope tied around her narrow waist and pulled up tightly between the soft folds of her labia. I saw Mora standing over her holding the rope and controlling her movements. I saw myself taking her place when she became tired. I pictured myself kneeling down in front of him, letting him tie the rope around my waist, and then opening my legs slightly as he pulled it between them. I felt its roughness, the hairiness of the course hemp, and felt the moisture as it ran from me and made the rope wet. I felt the hardness of the floor against my hands and knees and saw Mora's shiny black shoes in front of my face as he stood over me and observed my work. I felt the overbearing presence of my master, the obligation that went with my servility and the thrill of acting as the direct result of another's will. I kept my head down and rubbed the cloth as hard as I could across the wet floor, trying to do the best job possible, hoping for his favour, for his approval. I imagined Galen entering and watching me work. He would look pleased and smile as Mora greeted him, but I would not stop cleaning the floor and I would not look up in case Galen thought I was being lazy...

The images thrilled me and I wanted to unclasp my hands and slip my fingers across the back of my upturned thighs and press them against my vulva. It was squeezed tightly between my legs, which were crushing my breasts, my knees against my forehead, and I stayed that way all night. I had no way to mark the passage of time, but at least one whole night must have passed. It could have been a small eternity I spent in the dark, curled up like an embryo.

The next morning when the doors opened, I was shocked by the sudden light and at first my eyes refused to adjust. The day after that it was easier, and after a while, whenever he opened the doors, I did not flinch or show any surprise whatsoever. I felt quite the opposite, perfectly calm, as if the world outside the cupboard could no longer shock me, as if it contained nothing capable of surprising me. I did not get out reluctantly when he told me to, but when in the evening he took me back to the cupboard, I climbed in again with undiluted enthusiasm.

Most days I spent cleaning the house, other days I was made to serve Mora his meals on a tray. Once I worked with Cleo on the floor of the enclosed terrace, but we were not allowed to speak to each other. I listened to her as she shuffled beside me on her hands and knees, and felt a thrill of excitement as I heard

99

water draining back into her bucket as she wrung her cloth. Each night I was instructed to get into the cupboard and each night I stayed there, crouched in the centre section inhaling the scent of the fragrant timber and revelling in the images filling both my waking and sleeping mind. Sometimes I wondered if he would tell me to get into one of the other sections, but he never did.

I thought again of the flotation tank, of being suspended by my braid, of being lost in the beautiful sense of confusion, the mixing of fantasy with reality, the stretching of time and the overwhelming intensification of my senses. But captivity in the cupboard was different; it was more of a physical experience. In the tank I could feel nothing, but in the dark cupboard I sensed my environment and felt my discomfort. And as I relished the pressure of the top shelf against the back of my head, and the tension in my shoulders as I sat squeezed up with my arms around my legs, I experienced an irrationally intense pleasure. Each time I tried to move and could not, I cherished the strange gratification being constricted provided me with. But it was not just my inability to move I found so satisfying, it was the isolation and the knowledge of being trapped until my master released me. I did not know how long it would be until he opened the doors, and I did not crave for it to happen, for part of me did not want to be released. Not knowing when he would come and tell me to get out stoked my intense excitement. The tension of waiting lit the flames that, as the waiting continued, burned inside me delightfully. And the waiting, the open-ended anticipation always ended in a blaze of joy between my legs when he finally opened the doors again.

On the last night I spent in Mora's house, Juan Carlos arrived. I was tied up with rope and waiting on my hands and knees on the floor as Mora ate his meal. I looked up to see who the visitor was, but as soon as he sat down with Mora I dropped my gaze.

They spoke quietly together, but I did not listen to what they said. It was irrelevant to me. I simply wanted to feel the pressure of the floor against the palms of my hands and against my knees and the tops of my feet. I just wanted to feel the thrill inside me every time I glanced at the rope attached to me and resting on Mora's knee. Sometimes he tied the rope to the leg of the table while he ate and sometimes he tied it to the door handle. I did not know which I preferred, but I knew I felt disappointed when he undid it every night, and the feeling lasted until I climbed into the sanctuary of the cupboard again.

The two men shook hands as though agreeing to something, and then Mora rose and led me to a downstairs bedroom. He untied the rope, but even though I was free I still waited on my hands and knees. He took some clothes from a large chest of drawers and placed them on the bed. 'Wash and get dressed,' he said curtly, and left me alone.

I took a shower, soaping myself luxuriously and relishing the hot flow of water as it ran down over my body. Mora had laid out a long, light-blue satin dress, a white silk thong and a pair of blue high-heels. I slipped the thong on and pulled it tightly up between my legs. It reminded me of being tied up with the rope, but instead of the harshness of the rough hemp, my tender pussy was caressed and embraced by the silk, which was so soft I could barely feel the thin band stretching from the narrow gusset up between my buttocks to the delicate waistband. I slipped the dress on and it felt delightfully light and cool, clinging to my curves and hanging from my shoulders from thin straps. It was cut low; the top halves of my breasts were exposed. My feet slipped easily into the expensive leather shoes and the extreme heels accentuated my shapely calves. I smoothed the dress down over my hips, and then sat down on the edge of the bed and waited with my hands on my knees, my wet hair hanging down between my shoulder blades making me shiver as cool drops of water slipped beneath the dress and trickled down my back.

Mora and Juan Carlos returned and told me to stand in the middle of the room. They looked me up and down, and both seemed pleased by what they saw. Juan Carlos then led me upstairs and out into the street. I could not gage how long I had been in the house, but I felt anxious about being taken away from my daily captivity on the rope and my cramped nights in the cupboard.

Outside it was ominously dark, the atmosphere heavy with the moisture of an oncoming storm. Juan Carlos held my elbow and led me along the cobbled pavement. Every so often a sudden burst of humid wind whipped up from nowhere, blew across my face and died away just as swiftly. Ahead of us the dark-blue of the night sky glowed with a vast dome of light rising up from crowded open-air cafes, bars, and nightclubs. He led me from street to street and I revelled in the feeling of being pulled along like a captive. I imagined being bargained for, stared at and inspected. I wanted to be pushed into dark doorways or dark alleys and pressed against dirty walls while my purchasers took their pleasure from me in any way they chose. I wanted to experience the humiliation of being bought and traded. I wanted to feel the shame of not knowing what would happen to me in the hands of my new owners. I wanted to be completely at the mercy of others, to be used for their enjoyment, to be forced to submit to their will and treated not as a person, but as their sexual slave.

We came out into a busy square, ablaze with light and noise. He dragged me into it and I felt as if I was being pulled down into a cauldron of heat. People jostled against me, drinking, talking loudly, embracing and laughing seemingly all at the same time. They pushed against each other; scantily clad women brushing against lightly dressed men, each one excited by the novelty of fresh company, thrilled by the scent of unknown flesh. I picked up on their sense of expectation, breathing it in as wafts of perfume filled my nostrils and the noise of excited chatter flooded my ears. We pushed our way between the tangle of tables on the pavement, dodging waiters and the upraised arms of beckoning customers as we made our way into one of the noisy bars.

The smoky space was packed with people, and as I glanced across the sea of faces I thought I saw Cleo the way she looked the day I met her, throwing back her mane of blonde hair and laughing with bubbly joy, her white teeth neat and bright. I blinked, and when I looked again the girl had vanished, absorbed by the heat and smoke like a delicate phantom. I shivered and felt goose pimples on my neck as I realised how easily I could imagine everyone there was someone I knew... Eve was sitting quietly at a table, Mora was ordering drinks and Galen was speaking seriously to a small group of women as they listened attentively to every word he said... I shook my head in an attempt to clear my mind, and the pictures broke into a jumble of blurred, fragmented shards that fell away like shattered glass.

We walked to one side of the bar where there were several partially screened off tables. Juan Carlos pushed me behind one of the partitions and told me to sit at the small table. A waiter brought us drinks and Juan Carlos hung his arms over the top of the screen, looking around and waving to people he knew, shouting greetings into the almost deafening roar of conversation. I sat silently and sipped my drink. I felt uncomfortable from the heat, the noise and from being exposed to so many people after my time of isolation in Mora's house. Sleeping in a silent cupboard had lessened my ability to cope with the sort of clamour engulfing me now, and I wanted to return to my safe and quiet place. I wanted to return to the house and climb onto my shelf. I wanted to wait there, bent and cramped, until the doors were opened and I was let out, and then I wanted to work all day, led around the floor with the rope tied tightly to my waist and pulled up between my legs. I wanted to feel again the thrilling surge of delight as I wallowed in my absolute subservience. I wanted to feel the anxiety of being released from the rope, which was always replaced with pleasure as I climbed again into the dark and silent cupboard. But I stopped thinking about it. I knew why I was here. It was another part of my test.

Juan Carlos waved at a man standing nearby, encouraging him to join us. I did not like the look of him at all, and he had not shaved for several days. He leered at me as he walked behind the screen and shook hands with Juan Carlos. They spoke together in Spanish, the man glancing at me every so often, and each time he did I looked away. I looked around, wanting to be distracted, but from where I sat I could not see over the screen. Juan Carlos held up his hands with his fingers and thumb wide apart. The stranger shook his head and Juan Carlos pulled his thumb down tight to his palm. The man nodded in agreement.

Juan Carlos told me to go with the man and do whatever he demanded.

I stood up, and my new owner took my arm gruffly. His large hand was clammy against my skin, and when he pushed me forward I stumbled as one of my high-heels caught in the uneven floorboards. Juan Carlos looked at me sternly and I flushed with embarrassment. I felt guilty for being so inept, for showing a lack of poise. And I could not tell whether I was afraid or eager. This was what I had been dreaming about all those long dark nights in the cupboard. This was what I had imagined happening to me when I watched the girl being sold by the taxi driver in the alley. But now it was actually happening to me, I felt a surge of unexpected fear. I felt a chill travel down my spine as I saw my situation in the harsh light of reality. This was no illusion, no fantasy, this was really happening to me and I did not know whether or not I could go through with it.

I looked at the man who had paid money for me, and he smiled lecherously as he wrapped an arm roughly around my waist. I felt his strength as he guided me forward. It was like being carried along by a river in flood, caught in the pull of an irresistible current threatened on all sides by spinning whirlpools and deadly rocks. He led me through the crowd, pushing between people who did not bother to step aside and make way for us. They thronged around us, blocking my vision like a solid wall, their voices pounding in my ears and the lights and brightness all around pounding in my head until I thought it would burst. Everything was a blur, a cacophony of light and sound, and then suddenly we stopped, unable to pass beyond a tight knot of shouting, laughing revellers. A woman - her skimpy dress slit almost to the waist - pressed against me, and suddenly I felt a soft breath close to my ear and all the noise fell away to silence as Galen said, 'Syra, my pet, are you yet truly bad? Have you at last allowed your wickedness to take control or are you still a prisoner of fear?'

I felt the man pulling me through the crowd, squeezing my arm in an effort to drive me forward, but my master's question pinned me to the spot. I was suddenly lost in a dream; a reverie descended over me as I felt Galen's closeness, as I realised he was there, watching me, preparing me, testing me... 'I don't know,' I said without turning my head, hoping he could hear me. I hung there as if suspended, waiting for him to reply, to encourage me, to tell me I had achieved my goal, but I heard nothing. I turned my head in the direction I thought he was, but he was gone, vanished into the crowd as if he had never been there at all, as if he was not a corporeal form but a god or an angel visiting the earth only fleetingly and leaving as quickly as he came.

My buyer pressed me forward, and this time I yielded to his insistence. I did not hold back. I was suddenly filled with purpose, with need, and deeply exhilarated by the sense of Galen's approval.

The man pulled me into an alcove at the rear of the cafe and pressed me back against a roughly plastered wall. I could feel the course surface as he pushed my shoulders against it and smothered my lips with his. I dropped my arms to my sides and stared straight ahead as his tongue penetrated my mouth, probing, while his hands reached around and grabbed my buttocks through my dress. He lifted it impatiently to my waist, and then he grabbed me beneath my thighs and hoisted me up into his arms, wrapping my legs around his hips.

I gasped, slipping my arms around his neck and clinging to him as with one hand he held me up and with the other he pushed the gusset of my thong panties aside. He drove two fingers up into my pussy and made me ride his hand, keeping his mouth on mine and driving his tongue into it.

Then I felt the heat of his glans between my legs, searing the lips of my labia and spreading them open as the thick tip of his penis worked its way inside me, lifting me up on it. I tried to cry out, but his mouth stifled any sound I made as he fed his huge cock up inside me, thrusting it home. I was breathless and almost frightened of how stuffed I felt by his erection, which just seemed to keep getting bigger and harder, swelling and pulsing and filling me like no other penis ever had.

Then suddenly I stopped resisting and sacrificed myself to his magnificent shaft, sinking heavily and riding him, climaxing around his colossal hard-on as I felt it erupting into my fully stretched cunt.

My legs were trembling as I walked back into the cafe. I sat down at the table and Juan Carlos smiled knowingly at me. I blushed slightly and felt the heat of shame rising to my face. I sipped my drink, and saw its surface broken into a confusion of ripples by my shaky grip.

Two men came and joined us, and again Juan Carlos bargained with them in Spanish. I lowered my eyes as they talked, but I knew all the time the haggling proceeded that they were looking at me, determining how much I was worth. Suddenly one of the men reached under the table, pulled up my dress and grabbed my knee. He wrapped his fingers around it and squeezed as I tried to pull back, but he held it tight. He moved his hand up my thigh and his fingers touched the soft gusset of my thong, and I squirmed on the chair as he felt the wetness around my pussy.

Juan Carlos shook hands with the other man and nodded as banknotes were counted out. The crude fumbling between my thighs disappeared, and without speaking the two strangers led me through the crowd. This time I was aware of people staring at me. I sensed some of them knew what was happening. They knew I was being sold for sex. I tried to ignore them, but the way they smiled condemned me, and as I walked between them my two companions felt like silent guards leading me to the gallows.

One of the men, the taller of the two, pushed me forward through an open doorway into a small courtyard. I grabbed the door as I fell forward and it swung loosely on its hinges. There was a stained urinal in one corner of the yard and rubbish was piled up in another. The taller man grabbed me from behind, holding one arm around my chest and thrusting his free hand between my legs from the front. I did not know whether to struggle or not. I was not sure what was expected of me, what had been paid for, whether I should be compliant or whether I should fight back. Then he forced me away, pulling at my dress and lifting it up so he could thrust his hand down the front of my thong. He bent me forward as the other man knelt in front of me and undid his trousers. He held his cock in one hand and gripped my face with the other, and fed it swiftly into my mouth. I moaned repeatedly, as each time he thrust between my stretched lips his erection nudged the back of my throat.

'*Chupame!*' he growled, urging me to take it even deeper. I was not satisfying him, and I could sense their annoyance. I sucked harder, caressing my tongue against his ribbed shaft.

'*Chupame, cono!*' He pulled my hair as if that would help me understand what he wanted.

The other man held me firmly as he pulled my thong down to just beneath my buttocks. '*Puta,*' he hissed.

The first smack made me gulp and I nearly gagged as the man kneeling before me kept driving his cock down into my throat. I tried to pull away and the second blow was even harder than the first.

I was spanked repeatedly and each slap drove his friend's erection deeper into my straining mouth. I felt the heat of his hand on my buttocks, and also the heat of my own desire deep within. Then I realised he was no longer holding me, that I was bending forward without being forced to, my lips pressed against flesh as I deep-throated the erection between my lips, and I experienced my first orgasm as the man before me spewed his semen down my throat. Then I came again when I felt the second man ejaculating over my flaming buttocks.

Then they pulled me to my feet and barked at me to tidy myself up.

I felt dirty and defiled. My hair was tangled and there were wet stains on the front of my dress. I smoothed it down and ran my fingers through my hair as they pulled me back inside. But they let go of me at once, and panicking, I struck out on my own, fighting to find my way back to Juan Carlos.

He looked up at me and sneered. I wanted to ask him to take me back to Mora's house, but I could tell he was only thinking of one thing - selling me again.

The waiter brought more drinks and I heard the crowd beginning to thin out. A man and a woman appeared behind the screen. The man was slender and dressed in a grey suit with a white shirt and a dark-blue tie. He was also carrying a briefcase. The woman was also tall and slender with close-cropped black hair, and she was wearing a short black dress. Her eyebrows were no more than thin pencil lines, her cheekbones high and well defined, and her lips were a glossy red. Juan Carlos greeted them and they sat down. The woman did not look in my direction, but the man kept glancing at me as he spoke to my owner. He took out his wallet and counted notes onto the table. Juan Carlos picked them up and left as the man in the suit smiled at me.

'Take off your dress, my dear,' he demanded in perfect English. 'Slowly. I do not want to be short-changed.'

I stood up before them and took hold of my dress just below my hips. I lifted it slowly to my face and held it there, imagining again the stillness of the tank and the splendid isolation of the wardrobe. I knew they were staring at my body and my only purpose in life at that moment was to fulfil their expectations.

I lifted the dress further and pulled it free over my head. It fell loosely in my hands and I held it by my side for a while, standing naked before the couple except for my white thong and blue shoes. I exposed myself to the man and woman with my mouth slightly open, as if I was about to speak, as if I had thought of something to say, but I remained silent as he opened his briefcase, took out a rope and handed it to his companion.

I knew there was nothing I could say, nothing I could even think. The only thing to do was submit.

The woman got up and, holding one end of the rope in her right hand, dropped the other end rhythmically across the upturned palm of her left hand.

'Turn around,' she said.

I let go of my dress, turned around and gripped the top edge of the screen, looking over at the bar and a group of young waiters who had all paused in their work to stare at me.

I twisted sideways as the first lash fell across my back. The ends of the rope flicked around the sides of my ribs and burned like needles. But I knew I deserved to be punished, so I straightened my back in preparation for the next blow.

When it came it was even harder to bear, stinging my flesh and penetrating me with pain, but I took it, clinging to the screen. Each time the rope fell it landed on a different part of my back and buttocks, and each blow brought fresh images to my mind - what I had done with the first man, and then with the other two out in the courtyard - and each lash, each stinging scourge, filled me with remorse and contrition. I felt like a nun stretched out before a torturing abbess, rejoicing in every blow of the whip as each drove me closer to salvation.

In my mind I saw Galen, smiling at my penitence, nodding benevolently like a beautiful pagan god as tears of agony and joy streamed down my face.

After the couple finished with me, I leaned against the screen until I became aware of Juan Carlos staring at me. He made me sit down, and I squirmed uncomfortably on the hard seat. He looked at me reprovingly and I tried to keep still, but could not.

I lifted myself off the seat slightly, suddenly embarrassed by my nakedness, and as I sat back again I became shamefully aware of the warm wetness between my legs. He offered me a drink, and I bit my lip in a vain effort to stop my hand from shaking as I accepted it.

CHAPTER 13

He took what I had written and read it carefully, but watching his face I knew he would find it unsatisfactory. I sat and waited, my back straight and my bent legs spread wide apart in the hope that showing my pussy would please him. He shook his head as if he expected more, as if he had hoped I would do better. I felt a twinge of anxiety, but that was all it was, a twinge, a flicker, and it passed almost as soon as it came. I was surprised by my reaction and let my legs part further, pressing the outside of my knees against the floor until they hurt.

'I am disappointed in you, Syra. I don't think you will ever be completely cured. There is still more to say, I think. You have not told me everything, have you?'

'I will say it all when I write the next part,' I replied, and bit my lip. This was the first time I had spoken to him. My head spun and I felt as though the floor was slipping away from beneath me. I was seized with a breathless panic. I did not know what was going to happen. I looked down between my legs, trying to convince myself I had said nothing and it was only my imagination, but I knew it wasn't.

He looked at me for a long time. He seemed to be challenging me to speak again, silently urging me to say something that would displease him so he could punish me, willing me to fall into a trap. 'I will cane you,' he decided at last.

My stomach filled with nervous excitement and the feeling of misplaced guilt welled up within me again.

106

'Bend over, Syra, and present yourself to me, your hands holding your ankles. Stretch yourself so each strike of the cane reminds you of what you have to write.'

I bent over as he instructed and waited for the caning to begin. It seemed as though I had done this so many times - exposed myself to him, taking my punishment - but now I sensed the delightful humiliation drawing to a close. As the cane fell across my bottom each stinging blow reminded me of what I still had to say. Each smarting strike, each clenching of my buttocks, brought into my head the complete picture of my misdeeds. I saw it all now and knew what I had to tell, but I waited until he was satisfied I had been punished enough, and even then, after he finished, I waited, bent over in case he wanted to discipline me some more.

But he left, and I turned back to my work. He was right. I can sense the end of the story and I know now I have to tell it all. I am no longer ashamed, and I do not feel embarrassed he thought badly of my work until now, because he was wrong. Fear is draining out of me. I have lost the apprehension he aroused from the instant I saw him. I am no longer afraid of being caned, of being bound and left in the dark, of being imprisoned with no idea of when I will be released. I do not fear his sudden demands or his outbursts of temper. He is no longer the reason I am writing my story, and when I am finished with it, I might not even show it to him. All I want now is to finish it for myself.

The following day the taxi driver drove me out of the city. I could tell where we were going; I recognised the buildings as they thinned on the outskirts of the city. The low rolling hills with their craggy limestone escarpments felt familiar, and finally I knew what to expect as I glimpsed the collection of white houses huddled beneath the old stadium.

I didn't wait for the driver to open the door. I got out by myself and strode towards the arena. I walked into the dark entrance tunnel and felt the waft of heat blowing through it making my light dress cling to my perspiring body. The air energised me and I walked forward with increased urgency, swinging my arms purposefully, as if the wildly cheering crowd was shouting for me to make my entrance.

I stopped in the darkest part of the tunnel. There was a figure standing in the shadows ahead, his shape silhouetted against the light from the open arena beyond, the edges of his form blurred by an incandescent corona of illumination. It was Galen. I stopped for a moment, before walking straight up to him.

'Syra, my pet, come to me,' he said almost tenderly. 'Embrace me.'

I flung my arms around his neck and inhaled his refined masculine scent. I felt the warmth of his body and his long hair against the side of my face. I tingled all over as his arms tightened around my waist and I succumbed to his strength.

'Are you ready to resolve the conflict that lies within you?' he asked quietly. 'Tell me, Syra, can I set you your final task?'

'Yes, you can,' I gasped, still hugging him.

107

'Then first tell me what happened to you in the cafe last night. If you are to be saved from the prison of your own passions, you must reveal it all, every detail. Tell me.'

As soon as he had spoken, I realised what had happened to me was not complete until I told him. Everything done to me was like a chimera in the shadows, and could only be fully revealed in the mysterious light of his knowledge. The truth was brimming from me and I could not hold it back any longer. 'Juan Carlos took me there,' I began.

'Did you want him? Could you still feel the weight of his cock in your hand from the time before? Could you still feel the stickiness of his semen spreading between your fingers?'

'Yes, yes I could. And yes, I still wanted him.'

'How?'

'I wanted him to grab me roughly, to take me behind the bushes of a park we walked past and ravage me. I wanted him to force my legs as wide apart as they would go and drive himself into me without caring about my feelings, without worrying about my pleasure, just satisfying himself by using my body.'

'What would you have done as he came inside you?'

'I would have sensed it was about to happen, I would have felt the increase in tension, the hardening, the throbbing, the surge of heat, and I would have clung to him, lifting myself off the ground and letting him ride me as I hung beneath him.'

He pushed me back against the wall and held my arms straight down by my sides. 'What happened when you arrived at the cafe?'

'We sat at a table. The crowd was noisy and I felt exposed. I'd spent so many nights in the cupboard at Mora's house that I felt vulnerable in front of so many people. Juan Carlos brought a man to see me. He looked me over carefully...'

'Did you try to show him you were worth buying, Syra?'

'I'm not sure...'

'What did he do after he paid for you?'

'He took me to the back of the cafe.'

'And what did he do to you, exactly?'

'He kissed me, to start with. I held onto him, with my legs wrapped around his hips, squeezing my pussy around him as he fucked me.'

'What then, what happened next?'

'I sat down again with Juan Carlos and he agreed on a price for me with two other men. They led me outside to a small yard and they both had me.'

'Did they make you come?'

'Yes, I couldn't stop myself. Climaxes just kept flowing from me like a never-ending river.'

'How did you feel when they took you back into the cafe, Syra?'

'Used. Tired and used. I stood amongst the crowd and felt dirty. The feeling was so wonderfully intense.'

'And did you take more, my pet? Were you able to sacrifice yourself to more of your desires?'

108

'Yes. Next Juan Carlos sold me to a man and a woman.'

'And what did they do with you?'

'The woman had a rope, split at one end into thin braids. She told me to lean against the partition that screened us, where everyone could see.'

'And did you?'

'Yes, of course. I was positioned carefully against the screen and whipped.'

'What sensations did you experience as you were being beaten in public, Syra?'

'More than I can remember clearly.'

'Tell me. You must remember every detail.'

'But there was so much pleasure and pain it was almost more than I could bear. I thought I was going to pass out. My nerves were on fire. I was set ablaze with sensations with every blow. A lacerating pain that became more and more confused with pleasure penetrated every fibre of my being. My mind was filled with images of myself being beaten. I could see my naked body stretched against the screen with everyone looking at me. I saw them watching me flinch each time the rope swept down, and watching me shudder each time an orgasm gripped me. I heard my own cries as they listened. When the couple had finished with me, they left me there hanging onto the screen, moaning with delight.'

'Now, Syra my pet, *now* you are ready to release your wickedness. I can see it flooding inside you, simmering like a volcano, building up an unstoppable pressure and waiting to erupt.'

'Oh yes!' The poetry of his words excited me even more. 'Yes, I can feel it, but I need your guidance. Please help me release my wickedness, master.'

'I will, Syra my slave... I will.'

'Tell me,' I begged breathlessly, 'please tell me how.'

'But remember, if you do it, if you succeed in releasing your wickedness, you will face your evil side and the knowledge may overpower you. And if you fail, you will realise you are only capable of fantasising and the sense of disappointment that comes with this realisation may also lead to your emotional destruction. In either case, you run the risk of psychological collapse, either subsumed by your own dark side, adrift in a world of unquenchable sexual desire, or irrecoverably condemned to a life of frustration and despair.'

'Tell me what I must do,' I said without hesitation. 'I do not care what can happen, just tell me!'

He took my arm and led me from the dark tunnel into the underground maze beneath the stadium. The smell of animals filled the air and the snorting and stamping of bulls competed with the echoing roar of the crowd from the terraces above. We walked between the bullpens and made our way to the entrance of the arena. As we got nearer to it the brightness intensified. Sunlight reflected off clouds of dust kicked up by the anxious bulls, and against this radiant illumination a myriad of insects revealed themselves as multicoloured iridescent swarms.

Espartaco stood with his assistants against a heavily built wooden barrier, erected to prevent direct entrance to the bullring. The glistening lustre of the red, green and gold sequins on his suit competed with the beauty of the insects buzzing almost enviously above him, the dazzling silver and purple outfits of his assistants more dimly reflecting his ostentatious brilliance. He held his black two-cornered hat in his hand, tapping its hard brim against the gartered tops of his pink knee-high stockings. He turned towards us as we approached, his small pigtail silhouetted against the light, the buckle holding it glinting almost blindingly. He approached us, holding his hand out to Galen, and I looked down at the taut movement of his muscular thighs and calves, relishing the sight of his cock's heavy bulge squeezed into his tight black trousers.

The two men greeted each other in Spanish, Espartaco bowing low to Galen with an air of polite arrogance. They talked enthusiastically, the bullfighter flashing his bright white teeth in a broad smile and clasping Galen by the shoulders when he said something that made him laugh. His vitality and energy thrilled me. I wanted to be close to him, to feel his strength, his courage, his fearlessness. I remembered when I met him how he held me against the balustrade of the president's box, how he stood behind me, pressing his erection against my buttocks as he stroked my pussy. I wanted him again now. I wanted him completely.

'*Senorita*,' he said in his deep, velvety voice, turning towards me.

I was filled with excitement and anticipation. 'Senor Espartaco,' I replied, taking his hand and looking deeply into his dark eyes.

'Do you grant me your favour for the fight, *senorita?* My fortune will be made by your kiss.'

Galen laughed. 'Yes, Syra,' he said, 'perhaps you could promise him your favour. Only, of course, on the condition that he is victorious.'

Espartaco clasped Galen's shoulders and laughed again. 'There is no question about it,' he declared. 'If the *senorita* promises me her favour, then I will be victorious. Espartaco only fights for victory. Espartaco does not know what it is to lose. *Senorita*, your favour?'

I took his hand and nodded.

He stepped back and bowed low, touching his shin with the backs of the fingers of the hand holding his hat while his other arm bent stiffly behind his back. I felt a surge of power as he bowed before me. I felt like an empress receiving a seafaring explorer on his long awaited return. But then his strength and authority infected me and my own fantasy of power dissipated like a dream. He was not my subject, *I* was *his* subject, and his willing victim.

He withdrew, still bowing, as his assistants collected around him like a small army. The crowd roared, a fanfare sounded, and after a final flourish of his hat, Espartaco straightened up proudly and strutted out into the arena, accompanied by a roaring accolade from the spectators.

I stood watching, felt the loss of his departure, and my stomach clenched with fear and excitement. There was a rush of activity and we were ushered behind a protective barrier as a wild bull was released into the ring. The animal kicked out at the heavy timber walls and ran threateningly towards the brightly dressed

110

men as they mockingly waived coloured scarves and ribbons in his fiery eyes. The bull's anger increased and foaming spit flew from his mouth and nostrils as he was driven into an uncontrollable rage, while the terraces shook with the thunderous clamour of the howling crowd.

'Poor Espartaco,' Galen said scornfully. 'He has become convinced of his own prowess, but his conviction is a falsehood. He has only been pitting himself against bulls already doomed to be his victims, poor drugged creatures that could not see him clearly and could barely keep themselves awake. But now things have changed. He has met the last of the approved bulls. Now we shall see if he has become so accustomed to his feeling of courage that he has indeed become courageous. He will need to be, because this time his opponent is no tame creature, by any standard. He is one of the fiercest bulls ever to be brought to this arena.'

'Will he be safe?' I asked anxiously.

'That is up to him, and it is the same for you, Syra. You cannot know if your courage is falsely based or not. It is up to you how you face your fears.'

I leaned against the sturdy timber barrier and stared closely at Espartaco. I wanted to see him face his opponent. I wanted to see the look on his face when he realised the bull was braver, stronger, more challenging than any he had ever encountered. I wanted to see what he did, whether he held back in shock or whether he was filled with increased strength as the challenge induced a new and higher level of resolve in him. I wanted him by his actions to reveal to me the way out of fear into the realm of unrestrained passion.

I liked the feel of Galen watching me as I watched Espartaco facing the bull. The matador's poise was exquisite as he twisted on the balls of his feet and laid his flaring cape on the ground. He smiled at the crowd, and then looked towards me and bowed. He seemed impregnable, tested to the limit but unbeatable. It did not matter his previous victims had been unable to give him a proper fight. That was not important now. His victory today lay in his confidence, in his self-belief. I knew he was a victor. I knew he would stand before the crowd in genuine triumph.

The spectators roared as I slowly tugged my dress up around my waist and eased the gusset of my panties to one side. The heat of my pussy seemed to scald my fingers. I lifted myself up on my hand and felt perspiration forming on my chest and the back of my neck. I was on fire. I slipped my fingers beneath the material and tugged it even further to the side, getting it out of my way and making my soft flesh available. I stroked and caressed my sex lips, teasing myself, and then played idly with my clitoris. I moaned as I touched it and felt ecstasy brewing inside me - but it was not enough.

The shrieking of the crowd filled my ears as I walked beyond the heavy wooden barrier into the arena. I relished the glare of the sun in my eyes and its heat on my shoulders and felt imbued with its radiance. It was as though its heat and brilliance injected me with a new sense of life. I saw Espartaco in the centre of the ring holding his sword over the back of the bull's neck as he looked down at his victim, mesmerising him, defeating him with his courage. I walked

111

towards him, still holding my dress up, and still cradling the soft flesh of my pussy in my hand. I felt my labia moving against my fingers as I walked across the sandy space, and with every step I shivered in the intense heat beneath fresh surges of delight. I felt free of all my fears, emancipated from all my inhibitions and consumed by the flood of all my needs and desires. I was no longer a prisoner. My passion had been released.

The crowd howled as Espartaco claimed his victory. Then he turned towards them, thrusting his chest out and holding his bloodstained sword high above his head. He looked like a god to me as flowers showered down upon him - roses, gardenias and violets - a flurry of colour pouring like a dissolving rainbow from a cloudless sky, and covering the ring in a carpet of petals as a tribute to triumph. I walked through the sea of flowers, and as Espartaco swung around to show himself to the whole stadium he saw me approaching. He brought his sword down and rested the tip next to his feet, watching me, encouraging me closer, inviting me into his powerful orbit. I felt like his next victim, hypnotised by his gaze, overcome by his bravery. But I was not innocent quarry. I was willing game striding like a princess into the arms of her valiant prince.

I stopped and bowed my head, acknowledging his power over me, showing him I was under his control, and then I knelt in front of him, offering myself like the defeated bull, submitting to his wishes. The stadium reverberated with the thunder of stamping feet and clapping hands as I lowered my head further, exposing myself to him, and he slipped the tip of the sword into the back of my dress. I shivered with ecstasy and tensed with excitement as he drove the sword forward and sliced my dress down the back. I fell facedown across the sand, inviting him to cut through the rest of the delicate material. He bent slightly, slit the garment all the way to the hem, and then twisted the tip of his sword to pull it aside, exposing me. Apart from my white panties, I lay naked before him and the crowd.

I felt the soft caress of petals falling across me. I rolled over onto my back and gazed up at the matador in submissive adoration as he inserted the tip of the sword between the waistband of my panties and my vulnerable flesh. I felt the heat of the sunlit steel against the lips of my pussy as he twisted the blade, and cut through the flimsy undergarment, fully exposing me.

I dropped my head to one side and looked up into the thronged terraces. The crowd was shouting and screaming, stamping their feet and banging their fists on the wooden benches. I could not tell whether they were angry or elated and I did not care. I thought I saw Eve sitting in the president's box. Yes, I was sure it was her holding Mora's arm, and by her side sat Cleo, her white teeth flashing in the sunlight as she laughed and shouted along with everyone else. I rolled back over onto my belly and crawled to Espartaco's feet. I held his ankles and dragged myself close enough to lick his shiny leather shoes, my head pounding with the deafening crowd. Then, from the corner of my eyes, I saw dozens of men leaping over the barriers and running towards me...

112

I awoke with a start when I heard the door opening. I offered my finished manuscript to him, but he did not enter. I squinted at his shape filling the doorway, and then I saw someone else standing beside him - a taller, leaner figure with long hair. They spoke quietly together and he opened the door wider so they could both peer in at me more closely. Then I was left alone in the dark again.

When he came back later and I handed him my work, he took it and set it aside without reading it. I felt a sickening knot of nerves in my stomach. Had all this effort been for nothing? Had he at this late stage given up trying to cure me? Perhaps I had always truly been beyond help? I picked up the pages and pushed them at him, pressing them against his chest, but he ignored me. I leaned forward and kissed him, but he pushed me away.

'There is no more to do,' he said. 'Your story is finished. It has brought you here to this place and to this moment in time. I do not want to read any more. There is nothing you have written I do not already know. No, there is no more to say and I can do nothing more for you.'

CHAPTER 14

He left me for a while and I sat silently, doing nothing, wondering what would happen next. I did not feel better. I was still confused; nothing felt clear. My thoughts were shrouded by a thick mist, my feelings of expectancy lost in a fog of disappointment. But deep in the back of my mind I knew what he said was true. It was all over. The story had ended. It had brought me to this point in time and to this place and there was nowhere else to go.

I had finally remembered what happened to me in the bullring. I had suppressed the memory, but now the images and feelings and smells all came back to me... numerous avaricious cocks penetrating me while the hot sand chafed my naked flesh, the burning sun and glimmering explosions of semen blinding me as I was tossed from man to man like a rag doll pierced by endless erections... I could see it all now clearly, and I could understand why I buried the event so deeply in my subconscious. I shivered as memories flooded back, pictures filling my mind, showing what I had done and what had happened to me as a result. But I could also see now into the beginning of my salvation. I could feel Galen lifting me in his arms afterwards, cradling me against his comforting chest and carrying me out of the arena, back through the dark tunnel and placing me gently in the taxi. I could remember looking back and seeing him standing near the entrance, with Eve on his arm. I could remember staring through the car window in a daze, watching the wires dipping between the telegraph posts, seeing the outspread wings of birds gliding by in the deep blue sky. I could remember the feeling of relief when he brought me here, laid me down on the floor and bound my ankles. I could feel again the sense of deliverance that swept over me when he first beat me with the cane and the deep, comforting heat that filled me.

Now he will be coming again, perhaps for the last time. He has cared for me long enough. He has protected me from myself and now he will let me go. He has punished me enough, not with anger but with compassion, and he knows he can do no more for me. Yet my recovery is incomplete, I know it. I hesitate to say I am cured, but he must release me and I must face the world again. I wish I could still claim his protection, but I know I cannot stay here forever. I will no longer have the safety of being bound, tied like an animal, and locked away in a dark, safe cell. I must face the risk of being free, of facing again the wickedness that has been released inside me. I must walk out into the light.

When he returned, he held my arm and led me out of the dingy cell. I wanted to look back, but I did not. I could not remember when I had last seen sunlight, and as I emerged from the cellar I tilted my head back and closed my eyes as though bathing in it. When I opened them, I saw I was standing in the hallway of the apartment I had stayed in when I first arrived on the *Costa del Sol*. A wave of anxiety drenched me. I wanted to fall to my knees and let him put the collar around my neck again and hold me against his legs. I wanted to feel the tug of the lead, the safety of his power, but as my panic receded I realised my thoughts were nothing more than vague desires. They were pale reflections compared to the burning clarity of my self-awareness.

We walked through the French doors into the small, enclosed garden. I looked up into the sun again, and flinched. He picked up a wide-brimmed sunhat from the stone bench and set it gently on my head. A mottling of light and shade fell across my arms, and when I looked down I was reminded of the fact that I was still naked. The flecks of sunlight skimmed across my skin and played around my feet as though enticing me to dance with them. He drew me over to the bench, and I sat down. I felt unsteady on my feet and was relieved to sit. The warm stone made the flesh of my buttocks tingle.

The large wooden door in the enclosing wall opened and a man walked towards us. I squinted to see if I could make out his features, but he was no more than a silhouette in the bright light.

'Professor Lange,' my keeper said to the approaching figure, 'it's good to see you again. It has been some months now.'

I was seized with confusion and bit my lip uncertainly. I did not know what was happening. The figure stretched out his hand and my heart leapt into my throat because it was Galen. Yet my keeper - my old supervisor, Dr Baal - was calling him Professor Lange, the psychologist I admired so much. How could Galen be Professor Lange?

'Max, it is always a pleasure,' Galen said as they shook hands. 'How has the treatment gone? Is she recovered?'

'Not completely,' Dr Baal replied, talking as if I was not there. 'But I cannot help her any more. I have brought her back as much as I can. At least she feels pain again. But I cannot guarantee she can control her desires any more than she could the last time you saw her, in the arena.'

'You have caned her frequently?'

114

'Of course.'

'And spanked her?'

'Every day, and she has responded, but the episode in the bullring was too much for her. She was overcome by the experience. I think she will never be quite the same again.'

'Syra, my pet,' Galen said gently, 'look, your friends are here. See, not only has your old supervisor, Dr Baal, given up his time to care for you, but your other friends are here to help as well.'

I looked beyond him. More figures were arriving, moving out of the sunlight like phantoms. Eve walked to Galen and stood beside him, looking compassionately down at me. Cleo smiled at me warmly and flicked her long hair back over her shoulders, while holding Espartaco's arm. Then the girl I had watched in the alley stepped forward and offered me her hand. I shook it weakly, and looked up at Dr Baal for a moment, hoping he would explain, but as he smiled and handed me a drink, I realised I did not need an explanation.

I had been Galen's experiment all along. Everyone else was either an associate or a colleague he recruited to help set me up.

We all sat together in the small garden as the sun dipped behind the wall and draped us in the warm shadows of evening. I wondered how many of Galen's experiments had needed treatment when their desires overcame them. I wondered how many had survived and how many had failed, and into which category I would fall in the end.

It has been several weeks now since I left Galen and the others. I miss them in a strange sort of way, but I am glad to be free. Galen did not try to stop me from leaving. He seemed happy for me, as though he knew I needed to go, and as I sat in the back of the taxi, I did not look back. Instead, I gazed into the rear-view mirror and held the driver's dark, smouldering eyes. I asked him to stop the car just before we reached the airport. I did not want to leave without once more feeling the heat of his hand on my bottom, without once more squirming beneath a firm, unforgiving spanking.

Also by Syra Bond and available as paperbacks at AMAZON

The Roman Slavegirl
Trojan Slaves
Trojan Whores
True Confessions
True Confessions 2